CRAZY FOR A GEEK GIRL

NICOLETTE DANE

CONTENTS

Copyright	v
About the Author	vii
Sign Up For Nico's Mailing List!	ix
Crazy For A Geek Girl	1
Thank You	77
Get A Free Story	79
Field Day	81
Tiny House Big Love	83
Floats Her Boat	85
Give Me Some Sugar	87
Getting Down To Business	89
Restless On A Road Trip	91
Full Bodied In The Vineyard	93
An Excerpt: Field Day	95
An Excerpt: Tiny House Big Love	109

Copyright © 2016 Nicolette Dane

This book is a work of fiction. Names, characters, places, and incidents either are products of the author's imagination or are used fictitiously. Any resemblance to actual persons, living or dead, events, or locales is entirely coincidental. All rights reserved.

ABOUT THE AUTHOR

Nicolette Dane landed in Chicago after studying writing in New York City. Flitting in and out of various jobs without finding her place, Nico decided to choose herself and commit to writing full-time. Her stories are contemporary scenarios of blossoming lesbian romance and voyeuristic tales meant to give you a peep show into the lives of sensual and complicated women. If you're a fan of uplifting and steamy lesbian passion, you've found your new favorite author.

www.nicolettedane.com

SIGN UP FOR NICO'S MAILING LIST!

If you'd like to be notified of all new releases from Nicolette Dane and receive a FREE story, point your web browser to https://readni.co and sign up for Nico's mailing list right now!

CRAZY FOR A GEEK GIRL

My name is Annette and I work too much. I know that it's nobody's fault but my own, I know that if I just planned things a little better, maybe stuck up for myself a bit more, perhaps learned how to say "no," I could achieve a better work/life balance. I could hit the gym, I could keep my condo nicer, and maybe I could even find myself in a relationship. Ugh. Relationships. Sore subject with me, actually.

I don't mind telling you. Maybe you're a lot like me.

I work in a corporate environment. Don't get me wrong — it's not a beige-walled, windowless hell. Far from it. I work for a very successful financial services firm that manages multiple billions of dollars for some pretty large funds. University endowments, pension funds for large corporations, the personal wealth of some of America's richest people. I mean, our client list is damn impressive and I'd certainly wow you with it if I wasn't sure I'd get fired for sharing that information with you. No, I won't really get fired. The company is employee-owned. If you're here long enough, work hard enough, and show your commitment to the company, you become a partner. And I was well on my way to that.

So yeah, because we manage so much wealth and make so much money ourselves, we've got a very nice office. Top floor of a newer Chicago skyscraper. We've got the entire floor and it's all windows, looking out to the beautiful cityscape. The Loop, the lake, the river, and beyond. You can even see Wrigley Field from our office if you squint a little bit. I'm lucky to have such a great office.

But it can still be a corporate slog sometimes. And one of those little corporate nettles in my ass has to do with my relationship stuff.

See, I work in marketing and client relations and I have to deal with a lot of rich men. I'm a pretty young woman, sliding into my early thirties — not to toot my own horn or anything — and these rich men like to do the flirty dance with me and I, unfortunately, have to flirt back. It's part of my job, sadly. And none of this would be that bad if I actually liked men. But I don't. I like women.

Romantically, that is. I like women romantically. I'm a lesbian.

But because I'm kind of girly, a lot of people don't see it. I try not to judge them for any of that. People are a product of their culture, especially older people who are more set in their ways, and as much as I'd just like to be accepted for who I am, I'm also not an idiot and understand that progress comes slowly. Many of the people I work with know that I'm a lesbian. I told the president and founder of the company, Levi Gravonsky, about it and he had some thoughtful words on the subject.

"You're lesbian?" he reiterated after I told him. He made a scrunched up face, like it wasn't important to him, and he shrugged. I mean, Levi was a Latvian Jew and came from a history of persecution. He was born after World War 2, but he might not have been if his parents hadn't escaped the German occupation.

"Yes," I said. "I just wanted to get that out in the open because of my position."

"Netty," he said with a knowing smile, using my nickname that so many of my coworkers had grown accustomed to using. "I know it is unfair, but many of our investors are from an old school world. They may say things to you, perhaps sexist things, because you are a pretty woman. But do not let that faze you."

"Okay," I said, nodding along with his advice.

"Instead, let it bolster you," Levi went on. "Stay strong, stay stoic, as you can control nobody's feelings but your own. Just know that any troubles you endure in our world because of your sexuality will be rewarded tenfold, financially speaking."

"I understand," I said.

"Nobody in this company will care or judge your sexuality," he said. "We are a meritocracy and you come with a lot of merit."

"Thank you, sir," I said.

"The world will continue to progress," said Levi. "And when people your age are the age of our investors, all of these perceptions will have changed. More acceptance."

"I sure hope so," I said. He smiled.

"Do what you can," he said. "And don't let anyone bring you down."

So this is all a very long and convoluted way of saying that I have some difficulty in getting into a relationship. I don't meet very many woman like me in my line of work, I work a ton and don't really do the bar scene, and I was burned on the whole online dating thing a couple years back. I'll just say that it's far too easy and alluring for people to misrepresent themselves in their online profiles.

My goal as the new year has rolled in: work less and still be successful. Which, I hope, will lead me to a fulfilling relationship. I could sure use it.

SITTING IN MY OFFICE, the clock nearing 7PM, I sighed and held my head up with my hands, elbows on my desk, staring into a spreadsheet on one of my monitors, an investor database program running on the other monitor. Many of the lights were already out throughout our large office and the cleaning crew was beginning to start their evening job. I was the last one in the office on a Friday, still working, still trying to get my job done.

As my eyes remained trained on my screen, my brain beginning to fizzle, feeling my productivity drop, I heard a soft knock at the metal frame of my open door. Looking up from behind my computer setup, I spotted a pretty young woman, probably late twenties. Her long, brown hair hung loose around her head, flowing down over her shoulders. She wore a v-neck t-shirt, the neckline and sleeves a bit loose and wavy, along with dark blue matchstick skinny jeans. Over her face was a large pair of dark-framed plastic glasses. She smiled at me cautiously.

"Hi," she said. "I'm Henrietta — or, um, Henry — and I'm with your IT firm. Did you see the email about our project tonight?"

"Oh shit," I said. "I'm sorry, Henry. I totally spaced on that. I'm Annette."

"It's okay," said Henry. "There are a couple other machines in this part of the office I can do before yours. We're doing a full virus sweep of the entire office."

"I did get the email," I said. "I'm sorry that I'm still here. Just so much work to do."

"That's fine," she said. "Why don't you just yell at me in the next office over once you're ready?"

"You know what?" I said, pushing back from my desk. "It's Friday. I should just go home."

"Oh no," said Henry. "I'm not trying to kick you out. We have plenty of time."

"No," I said. "This is a great excuse for me to leave this stuff for Monday. Come on in," I said, waving her in. "Henry?"

"Yeah," she said. "That's me." She stepped further into

my office, her hands slid into the back pockets of her tight jeans. "You guys have a really nice office here."

"Thanks," I said, smiling at her. I couldn't help myself. I found her really attractive. She was geeky and it was endearing. Kind of like a hipster geek, you know? And it was really refreshing and cool to see a young woman as an IT computer consultant. I hadn't seen much of that in my time in the corporate world. "How come I've never seen you around the office before?" I asked, easing back into my desk chair and looking up at Henry.

"I'm usually not assigned to your company," she said. "You probably see Matt and Tim more often."

"Oh yes," I said. "I see them all the time."

"Our entire group is here to do the virus sweep," she said. "It's a lot of computers and it just goes faster with us all here."

"Makes sense," I said. "Does my computer have a virus?"

"No," said Henry. "Probably not. I haven't found one yet in the computers I've done. But we do it just as a precautionary measure because of the sensitive data you guys work with."

"Great," I said, standing up now from my chair. "Do you want to take over?"

"Sure," said Henry, sliding around my desk and navigating into my chair.

"Sorry about the shoes," I said. Underneath my desk I had put together a nice collection of footwear.

"I see it all the time," said Henry. "I'm not offended."

"Good," I said with a smile. As Henry leaned in to my computer, she inspected the programs I had open and then looked up to me.

"Mind if I close all this stuff out?" she asked. "I'll save any unsaved work."

"Okay," I said. She quickly and expertly went ahead, closing out my various windows, clicking save, shutting down my email, taking us back to my empty desktop.

"I love how you only have a couple icons on your desktop," said Henry with a smirk. "You wouldn't believe how many people have a desktop totally full of icons. It's a mess."

"I've seen that," I smiled. "I can't handle that kind of mess. I'm too orderly. It would drive me crazy."

"Me too," said Henry without looking up. She clicked around on my computer, bringing up a couple of programs, choosing options, clicking checkboxes. It was like she had done this a thousand times before because she most likely had. After a minute or so of navigation and choices, silent but for the clicking of the mouse, a window appeared on my computer indicating that a scan was in progress. Once the scan window was up, Henry sat back in my chair and smiled at me. "Now we wait."

"That's it?" I said.

"That's it," she said. "If this thing finds anything, we'll run some deeper scans. But if it comes up empty, we're done."

"Not bad," I said. "Pretty easy job."

"This is the easy part of it," she said. "It can get rough sometimes."

"I can imagine," I said. I stood there next to my desk, silence falling over the two of us as we'd sort of already exhausted conversation about Henry's purpose for being there. I wasn't ready to leave just yet, as I was eager to talk further with her and find out if, you know, she was like me. "Tough that you're working on a Friday night," I said, immediately unhappy with my conversation prompt. But it was already out there, so I had to run with it.

"Nah," said Henry. "I mean, I'd probably just be gaming or something otherwise."

"Gaming?" I asked. "What do you mean?"

"I don't do the whole Friday night afterwork party thing," she said. "I usually get together with a group of people online and play a game."

"Really?" I said. "What game?"

"Battle Guildstrike," Henry said, somewhat bashfully. "It's an MMORPG — er, a massively multiplayer online role-playing game. Super nerdy, I know."

"I think I've heard of it," I said. "It's a pretty big deal, right?

"Yeah," she said. "It's fun. You get to build a character and play a basically never-ending game with millions of other people all over the world."

"So that's how you spend Friday nights?" I asked. "You don't go out with friends, or like, a boyfriend, or something?"

"No," she said, her eyebrows shifting upwards at me skeptically. "Not my scene, really."

"I'm sorry," I said. "I didn't mean to imply anything." Though, you know, I pretty much did. Just digging, that's all.

"That's all right," said Henry, looking into the computer monitor, clicking a few windows with the mouse, checking the various status indicators. The look on her face made it seem like she was almost done with me.

"Look," I said. "I didn't mean to pry about your personal life or anything," I said. "I just don't get out much either. I work all the time. Isn't it apparent?" I hung my arms out, indicating the obviousness as I was still at work on a Friday night.

"Yeah," said Henry, her face turning toward me once more. She offered me a knowing smile.

"Maybe since you're here working and missing your usual game night," I began. "And I'm still here, wrapping up my work, maybe we could go catch a drink downstairs when you're all finished up and just, I don't know, talk…"

"I don't really drink," said Henry.

"Neither do I," I said. "It's just a thing people do. I was going to have a ginger ale."

"How about tea?" she said.

"What?"

"I know of a good teahouse that's open late," she said.

"Tea would be great," I said happily. "I have a car and can drive us."

"Cool," said Henry with a soft smile. "Let me finish up a few more computers and it's a date."

WE GOT a parking spot on the street directly in front of the teahouse that Henry had recommended. She had remarked about how nice my car was, a Mercedes SUV, and I felt a little self-conscious about it the entire ride. I know I shouldn't have been embarrassed about making money, but Henry and I were from different worlds. Despite the fact that she worked for an IT consultancy that serviced corporate clients like my company, she was still a little bit counter-culture in her geeky hipness. She was just getting started in her career, and I was beginning the rise to the top of mine.

After rushing from the car to the teahouse, braving the January cold, the two of us busted into the door and were hit with a comforting warmth. The teahouse was casual and laid-back, comfortable couches and cushions, red tapestries and flowing drapes abounding in the cafe. It was a long space, looking as though there were two rooms in the teahouse. There were other people there, but by no means packed on this wintry Chicago evening.

Henry ordered tea for both of us and then lead me over to some cushions on the floor, separated by a low table. I honestly felt a little out of place in my corporate casual attire, while Henry fit right in looking relaxedly bohemian. After taking her wool coat off and letting it slide to the floor against the wall next to our seating area, she let her scarf remain around her neck and adjusted her glasses with a smile in my direction.

"Do we have to go up and get the tea?" I asked. "Or should we just sit down?"

"We can sit," she said, sitting down onto the cushion. "They'll bring the tea over."

And it wasn't much longer until the tea was delivered by a young guy with a thin beard and long hair twisted up in a bun. The two of us smiled up at him as he squatted to place the tea on our table, thanking him.

Henry poured our small cups full from the white ceramic kettle, being careful not to spill.

"This is dragon pearl jasmine," she said. "It comes in little hand-rolled pearls. Very floral and sweet."

"I have to say," I said, picking up my cup and taking a small sip. "I didn't expect to end up at a teahouse after work on a Friday. But I'm happy I'm here," I said with a smile. "It's good." I lowered my cup back to the saucer on the table.

"Yeah, it's one of my favorites," said Henry.

"So don't be offended," I began, tilting my head to side and wondering if I should actually say what I was about to say. "Are you, like, a geeky hipster type girl?" Henry laughed.

"Yeah, I guess," she said. "I'm just who I am, though."

"I know," I said. "I don't mean to try to fit you into some box. I just don't get much social interaction these days so I'm a bit out of touch."

"It's cool," said Henry. "I'm not mad. But it does prompt me to want to ask you a question."

"Go for it," I said with an accepting grin. "Ask away."

"How old are you?" she said. "That's not rude, is it?"

"No," I said. "That's fine. I'm 34. How old are you?"

"I'm 27," said Henry. "Not that far apart."

"No," I mused, both the tea and Henry's demeanor warming me up. She looked really cute sitting across from me in her thin little t-shirt and scarf. I couldn't help but give a bit of a blushing smile as I looked at her.

"I like your name," said Henry. "It was my grandmother's name. And Henrietta was my other grandmother's name."

"That's an interesting coincidence," I said. "I go by Netty to my friends."

"That's really cute," chuckled Henry. "That's a cute nickname for Annette."

"Yeah, my parents always called me that and it stuck," I said.

"I started going by Henry in college," she said. "I guess Henrietta just felt too girly to me."

"Well, going by Henry swaps that," I said with a small laugh. Henry smiled.

"Yeah," she said. "Maybe a little too far away. But I don't think about it anymore. It's just my name."

We shared a moment of silence in the conversation. That's how it always is, isn't it? That awkward, getting-to-know-you conversation is usually peppered with some silence as you consider what's next.

"Is it weird to be out with a client of yours?" I asked. "I don't mean to make it weird by saying that, I'm just interested."

"A little," said Henry. "But not really. Everything is a

little weird to me, so I guess that makes nothing weird ultimately." We both laughed softly together.

"I guess that's a good attitude to have," I said. I brought my cup up and took a sip of tea.

"Hey Netty," said Henry, chewing a bit on her lip. "I have a hunch and I just want to get it out there."

"All right," I said.

"You're a lesbian, right?" she said. Her face was trepidatious but serious.

"Yes," I said. "I am."

"Okay," said Netty. "I mean, I thought you were. I just wasn't totally sure." Netty removed her black frames from her face and wiped the lenses off with her t-shirt, then replacing them back atop her nose.

"Are you?" I asked cautiously, widening my eyes.

"Mm hmm," she affirmed.

I suddenly felt a great sense of relief. I was uncertain up to that point about Henry. I didn't want to offend her or get into an awkward situation. Smiling to myself, I pressed on and tried to remember how to better flirt. It had been a while for me.

"What got you into computers?" I asked. Henry looked away and her face showed a bit of embarrassment.

"I just…" she began. "I've always been a bit of a computer geek. Throughout my teenage years and stuff. It was natural for me."

"That's cool," I said. "It's impressive. I'm all right with them, but definitely not good enough to do what you do."

"It's pretty easy for me," she admitted. I could tell talking about her nerdiness made her shy.

"I think it's great," I said, reaching across the table and lightly touching her hand. Henry's eyes slowly returned to our conversation and I could tell she was blushing.

After finishing our tea, Henry admitted to me that she was scheduled to play her game later that evening and had to head home. As we hung together near the doorway of the teahouse, we exchanged numbers and my heart fluttered. I was feeling rather infatuated with her. In that moment, I was glad we hadn't gone out for drinks because I knew I would have been tempted to drink, tried to press her into hanging out even later, with the idea of perhaps accelerating things too quickly. I knew myself well and that was one of the reasons I tried to avoid drinking alcohol. The teahouse had been a wonderful option.

"It was nice getting to know you, Netty," she said, leaning forward and hugging me.

"You too," I said, returning her hug. "Maybe we could get together again sometime?"

"Totally," said Henry. "Text me."

"All right," I smiled, shaking my phone before slipping it into my pocket. "Oh, do you need a ride?"

"Naw," she said. "I live just a couple blocks away. I guess I sorta tricked you into driving to my neighborhood." I laughed.

"Are you sure?" I reiterated. "It's cold."

"I'll be fine."

"Okay," I said. I couldn't help myself and I leaned in to

hug her again, our big soft winter coats pushing against one another as we embraced. "Stay warm."

"Have a good night," said Henry with a smile, giving me a little wave before slipping a wool cap on her head and pushing out of the teahouse door, walking into the chilly winter evening, disappearing quickly into the darkness.

I sighed to myself. I missed Henry already and the usual loneliness began to set in.

I HAD a difficult time sleeping that night and woke up early rather than hazily remaining twisted up in my blankets. My mind was dwelling on an amalgam of issues, most notably my work project and my little tea date with Henry. After sleeping on the issue, I felt as though I had somewhat stepped around the line of professionalism by going out with her. While our time spent together was innocent enough, I couldn't help but think about making a go at her. There was something quite endearing to me about her geekiness. It was a world I had no experience with, outside my purview, and something that, admittedly, excited me greatly. I wanted to know more about her.

I looked around my bedroom, with it's modern design and large window wall, happy that I had been able to build such a life for myself and saddened that I didn't have someone next to me in bed to share it with. Maybe that person was Henry. I didn't know. But I so desperately wanted to find out.

With my hair back in a ponytail, wearing a white tank top and loose grey sweatpants, I gripped onto my phone and wandered into my kitchen. Coffee was already made thanks to my preprogramed coffeemaker — hey, I'm not totally tech illiterate — so I grabbed a cup and sat down at my kitchen island. I gazed into my phone and considered texting Henry, despite how early in the morning it was. I mean, a text at 7AM wasn't crazy on a Saturday morning, was it?

With that morning jolt of caffeine from my coffee, I worked up the courage to begin composing a text. I didn't really know what I could say but I just wanted to reach out, I just wanted a bit of a connection. I tried not to expect much of anything, I only felt like I needed to make a move.

"Thanks for the tea date last night," I began typing into my phone. "If you're free, maybe I could take you somewhere today?"

I stared down at my phone at this message in the composition window, feeling a bit scared to send it. Why was I scared? Why was I so nervous about this? It's not like I totally embarrassed myself the previous night. We got along great. I couldn't help but feel a little strange about our business relationship, but it wasn't like she was assigned to work at my company every day like some of her coworkers. I could navigate this. I was a professional success. Relationships didn't have to be so hard.

My finger dangled over the "send" button for a moment or two before I closed my eyes and finally touched the button. I took a deep breath, sat my phone on the counter, and watched the window to see if she'd text back.

I tried to imagine what I'd tell Henry we could do. Maybe we could go to the Natural History Museum or go take a cold walk along the lake. I guess the cold lake walk wasn't too enticing of a scenario, but I did enjoy seeing the lake in winter, snow all around the beach, frigid waves crashing up onto the shore. Although Chicago could get pretty grey in the winter, the lake was always a beautiful sight to behold.

Maybe we could go ice skating in Millennium Park? I mean, it sounds fun but it was a bit of a corny idea for a date. Very romantic comedy movie. I had a feeling that Henry might roll her eyes at the suggestion. I don't know why I thought that. Probably just projecting my own insecurities.

After I finished my cup of coffee and Henry still hadn't texted back, I felt a little distraught. Standing up from the stool at my kitchen island, I placed my empty cup in the sink and stretched out. Having no plans for the day, I figured I should just go hop into the shower, get dressed, and head in to the office. I could probably get a lot done with the quiet of a Saturday, as only a handful of the foreign market traders would be in to work. I wouldn't have to totally dress up, I could be comfortable and casual. And then maybe I could lighten my load for Monday.

Just as I made my move to leave the kitchen and head toward the shower, my phone buzzed on the counter and I almost tripped on my own feet as I leapt toward it excitedly.

How quickly our focus can change. I eagerly held the phone in both hands, unlocked it, and looked into the text window to gobble up Henry's response.

"Yeah!" was her response with a little yellow emoji smiling next to her text. "Still in bed, but totally down to hang later. What did you have in mind?"

I hadn't really settled on a date idea, so my brain began to race at a mile a minute. We could do brunch, I thought, and then off to something else. But what could that be? I wanted to make a good impression, like I was cool, like I had my act together, like I wasn't some lonely workaholic. I mean, I was a lonely workaholic but I didn't have to act like one when trying to impress somebody. I just couldn't get my mind straight or flesh out an idea.

After a moment, I just started typing to see what would come out.

"How about brunch?" I wrote, sending it in its own message first. I then furiously typed my next line into the phone with my thumbs. "Then maybe we could go ice skating downtown."

I felt my stomach drop after hitting send. I felt so unbelievably corny for suggesting ice skating. It could be fun, of course, but I felt like it made me seem old or something. Henry probably just wanted to camp out in her apartment with a blanket wrapped around her playing a computer game.

"Wow!" she typed back. "I would never have thought to do that. I'm in!"

My jaw about dropped when I read her text. Henry was

actually enthusiastic about my silly plan. But I was elated and relieved. I just hoped I remembered how to skate.

"I'll pick you up at 11," I wrote. "Text me your address."

It had been so long since I'd been on a Saturday day date. It didn't seem like this was my reality. But Henry had me feeling giddy again, giddy in a way that I hadn't felt in a long time. Since I'd cleaned up my act, gotten serious about work, love had become a difficult thing for me to wrangle. I wanted to really try to make things work with Henry, if she'd have me of course, and I was eager to impress. But how does someone like me impress a geek girl?

AFTER AN AMAZINGLY SOCIAL and animated brunch, we hopped into my SUV and drove downtown to Millennium Park to try this skating thing out. At the brunch spot they had mimosas on special, an unlimited mimosa deal, which I would have jumped at in a past life. I admit, I was still a little tempted but when I saw Henry decline the deal with a roll of her eyes, I knew it would be easy for me to say no as well. I couldn't help but smile as we hung out together, hoping I didn't look too stupid or anything, too eager, too infatuated.

The ice rink was bopping with people, bundled up figures gliding along the surface, scarves flying behind them, some people slipping and falling down on their butts with a laugh. It must have been twenty years since I last ice skated and I was definitely nervous. As we picked up our skates from the rental counter, Henry admitted something to me that made me even more nervous.

Flipping her scarf up over her shoulder and shrugging off a bit of cold, her dark glasses lightly fogging up as her warm breath drifted up her face, Henry grinned at me showing off her bright teeth.

"I used to be an ice skater," she said.

"What?" I exclaimed. "Are you serious?"

"Yeah," she said, looking demurely downwards for a moment. "I skated pretty seriously until I was 18 or so. It ended in college."

"Like competitions and such?" I asked.

"Yes," she admitted. "I should have told you at the restaurant but I was still a little embarrassed by it."

"You're embarrassed by it?" I scoffed with a teasing smile. "I haven't skated in a couple decades and I was never any good."

"We can just glide along the edges of the rink," said Henry, sitting down on a bench and slipping on her skates. I followed her lead, the two of us tying up our skates together, boots to the side.

"Okay," I agreed with a bit of hesitance. "Make sure I don't fall." Henry smiled, took up both of our boots, walked on her skates to the rental counter, and handed them over. Turning back to me, she opened her arms.

"Let's do it!" she said.

Although I had definitely been nervous, my skating legs came back to me after only a couple of minutes. It's amazing what the body can remember and do. Henry was obviously quite good, but she didn't flaunt it. Rather, the two of us slowly skated together along the edge, skating in time with some of the other people, moving deliberately, chatting and laughing as the winter sun peeked through the grey clouds above us, glimmering a reflection off the ice.

"We haven't really talked about what you do," said Henry, quickly skating ahead of me, deftly turning, and then lining back up with me again. "Obviously I know that you guys are an investment firm. But what do you do there?"

"I work in marketing and client relations," I said, sticking my tongue out, trying to insinuate that it was boring or no big deal. "It's fine. It's lucrative. But there are hurdles, like any job I suppose."

"Like what?" she asked.

"It's just a ton of work sometimes," I said. "It's taken over my life. I need a break from it."

"So why don't you just take a break?" said Henry, reaching out to steady me by grabbing my arm when she sensed I was losing my balance. Even after keeping me upright, she continued to hold onto me and we skated along together.

"I have a lot of responsibility," I said. "Hey, can I tell you something?"

"Yeah," said Henry. "Of course."

"I haven't said this out loud to anyone yet," I said. "And I know we just met, so don't think I'm weird."

"Oh jeez!" said Henry with a laugh, causing her glasses to slide down her nose a bit. She quickly reached a gloved hand up to adjust the frames on her face. "Don't put a ton of pressure on me or anything."

"Ugh, you're right," I said. "Forget it."

"No, I'm sorry," she said, tilting her head at me and smiling acceptingly. "Go ahead. Open up."

"Okay," I said, taking a deep breath, trying to remain upright on my skates, unsure as to why I was even admitting this to Henry. We had only just met and here I was, immediately moving to the heavy stuff. But I wanted this to all start out right, open and honest, and I was just coming to terms with what I was about to tell her myself.

"Your face changed," said Henry, her smile waning. "If you don't want to say this to me, Netty, you don't have to. You can wait and tell me some other time."

"No," I retorted. "No, I want to say this."

"All right," said Henry, tightening her grip on my arm to both stabilize and comfort me, bracing against me, keeping us both on our feet. The two of us looked ahead as we skated, Henry giving me some visual space so I didn't have to look her in the eyes with my admittance.

"I think my job gave me a problem," I started. "A problem with drinking."

"Oh," said Henry softly. "I understand."

"I don't want to make this too heavy or anything," I said. "I just wanted you to know. I'm in the process of giving it up. Giving alcohol up."

"That's great," said Henry, her smile returning. She looked to me and gave me a gentle glance, an understanding glance. "You'll be better for it."

"It's been tough," I said. "But I've been good! That teahouse last night was a total lifesaver. I can't believe I suggested going to the bar with you."

"Old habits die hard," she said. "Like I told you last night, I don't really drink. I mean, I'll occasionally have a glass of champagne or something at a wedding or an event but I don't really like it. I just do it to make other people happy. I usually can't even finish the drink!"

"Wow," I said, huffing out a warm breath into the cold air, confused and surprised by Henry's ability to abstain. "I want whatever you have." Henry laughed softly.

"I don't know how I do it," she said with a shrug. "I've just never really been interested in drinking."

"Thanks for letting me get it out," I said, relieved at how supportive Henry was being. "You know, it's kind of taboo to admit you're wrestling with alcohol. It makes the people you talk to about it question their relationship with it and that can be uncomfortable."

"Why do you think your job gave you this problem?" she asked.

"That's just my excuse right now," I said. "It helps me."

"Okay," said Henry, smiling.

"Thanks for listening," I said. "And thanks for not letting me fall."

"Hey, if you fall," she said, still gripping tight to me. "We both fall."

"So this is my place," I said, pushing the door open to my condo and letting Henry walk in first. She scooted her boots along the doormat to dry them off, then stepped over to the side and untied them. "Can I take your coat?"

"Sure," she said, unbuttoning her black wool coat and then turning around, allowing me to help slide it off her shoulders. I hung it up in the closet along with my own coat. I casually slipped out of my boots as well and the two of us moved together along the hard wood floors as I showed her my condo.

Henry looked so completely alluring to me. She wore thick black winter-weight leggings with a grey pair of shorts over top of them and a dark blue long-sleeved henley shirt, loose and billowy like it was a size too big for her, all the buttons at the neckline unbuttoned and causing the neck to open up wide and show off a white ribbed tank top underneath. Her black plastic glasses still had a bit of fog on them from coming indoors, and she adroitly removed them from her face and wiped them off on her shirt in a totally cute, unabashed way.

When I was younger — hell, even when I was Henry's age — I probably would have been snotty around a girl like her. Growing up I was popular, pretty, outgoing, and that lead to a bit of pretentiousness that followed me to college and into my adult working life. In fact, I know for certain that I had made fun of girls like Henry before, to their faces even, for being different, liking different stuff, acting kind of odd. At 34, I can definitely see how silly that all was. It especially got strange for me when I accepted that I was a lesbian. I really got confused about who I was.

A lot of my old friends abandoned me when I came out. When that happened, I realized that they were never really my friends to begin with and I would have been a lot better off in my youth and upbringing had I hung around more people like Henry. They always seemed to have it together. They never really cared what people thought of them, they just tried to be happy for themselves. All while we, the so-called "popular" kids, tried desperately to fit in, to be liked, and to not cause too many waves among our peer group.

"Would you like some coffee?" I asked. "Espresso?"

"Tea would be nice," said Henry. "This place is amazing, Netty."

Her summary of my condo made me feel a bit awkward. It was true that I lived in a pretty upscale place, one of the benefits of making a good wage and working in financial services. I knew I shouldn't be embarrassed by my success but I didn't want to make Henry think I was trying to impress her, you know? I was just being me.

"Tea," I repeated. "Sure thing!" Waving Henry along, we walked together through my modern-styled living room and into my kitchen. I put a small glass kettle on the burner, already filled with enough water for a couple mugs of tea, and turned on the heat.

"I'll be so embarrassed for you to see my apartment," said Henry. "It's a studio the size of your living room."

"Come on," I half-whined, looking away. "It's no big deal."

"This place is just beautiful," Henry mused, stepping away from me and toward a floor to ceiling window in the dining area next to my kitchen. I lived near Lake Michigan and looking out of the window you could see for miles into the lake. "The only way it could get better is if you had a computer battlestation right over there," she said with a grin, pointing. "Dual video cards, quad-core processor." I laughed.

"Yeah, but then you'd ignore me," I said.

"No, I'm just playing around," said Henry. "Half playing." She smirked with her correction.

Pulling the kettle off the burner, I filled our mugs and dropped a teabag in each. Together we picked up the mugs and moved out of the kitchen and toward the living room, sitting down next to each other on the couch. I really just enjoyed being with Henry. Being in her company. Being with her made me feel far less lonely, it took my mind totally off of work, and it made me feel like a human again.

Henry sat cross-legged on the couch, our bodies only about a foot apart, and she faced me as she held her tea in her lap, warming her hands on it. Her smile was humble, almost timid, as though she were waiting for me to start the next topic of conversation.

"I'm glad we're together," I said finally, feeling shy, looking away. "I don't have many friends anymore. Most of them got married, had kids, moved to the suburbs. It's weird, when you live a life opposite of the norm, all the people you used to be so close with eventually gravitate away from you."

"I've always been outside the norm," said Henry. She laughed at herself. "And many of my friends I met on the internet."

"How do you normally spend your time?" I asked. "When you're not working."

"I game," she said. "I read. I go to the teahouse and sketch. I'm actually thinking about getting into rock climbing."

"Rock climbing?" I repeated with a bit of surprise. "We're in Chicago, where are the mountains?" Henry snickered at me.

"No Netty," she said. "They have rock climbing gyms. It's a big wall with grips and holes and stuff on it, to simulate like you're climbing a mountain."

"That's wild," I said. "I can't believe I've never heard of that before. I'm not that out of the loop."

"You should come with me," she said, lightly sipping at her tea but quickly pulling back because of the temperature. "I've never done it before so we can both try it for the first time."

"It does sound interesting," I said, leaning over to take the teabag out of my mug, setting it down on a saucer. "I've never even considered it before."

Just then I heard my phone make a ding from across the room, buried in my purse.

"Is that you or me?" said Henry.

"Do we have the same tone?" I said.

"Yeah, we must," she said. "My phone's in my coat pocket."

"I bet it's me," I said, standing up from the couch and slinking over to the table near my front door. Fishing into my purse, I retrieved my phone and looked at the screen. "It's me," I said. I frowned as I read the text.

"You okay?" she asked as she noticed my face.

"Just work stuff," I said.

"Yeah, I hate getting those texts on a Saturday," said Henry. "Being in IT, I get them at all hours. My job has a tendency to be 24/7. I get so many automated emails at all hours, I can't even have my phone alert me to new messages. It would be dinging every couple minutes."

"I think I'm just going to ignore this," I said, flipping my phone to silent and stuffing it back into my purse. "It's not urgent and I'm having too good of a time with you."

"Aw," said Henry sweetly. Lifting her tea, she sipped, then set the mug down on the coffee table as I began walking back over toward her.

"They're talking about making me a partner," I said, approaching the couch and crumbling back down on it. "A lot of responsibility." I sighed. "You ever take an objective look at your life and think, boy, this just isn't where I saw myself?"

"Eh, I don't know," said Henry with a shrug. "I just kinda roll with it. I don't mind my job."

"I think it's more than that," I said. "More than just liking or disliking your job. It's a different clarity I'm coming upon."

"It's going to be fine, Netty," she said, her eyes beaming at me from behind her big frames. It was then that I really noticed her eye color. At first I thought it was blue, and maybe it was blue in certain lights, but there in my condo it was more of a steel blue, grey even. It was almost like it was absent of color, like her eyes existed in black and white while the rest of her was colorized. "At least you're beginning to see all of this," she continued on. "So many people go through life just accepting whatever, letting decisions be made for them, and that can only lead to dissatisfaction."

"Wise beyond your years," I mused. I smiled warmly at Henry and let my hand fall to her knee, giving her a gentle pet. She beamed at me, obviously enjoying the affection, the touch.

"I've really enjoyed our day so far," she said, watching me stroke her knee. "Do you have plans tonight?"

"No," I said. "Do you? Do you have to play your game?"

"I should," said Henry with trepidation. I could see her mulling over the options in her head. "I'm scheduled for a raid but I can cancel that."

"Are they going to toss you out of the group?" I said teasingly. I grinned impishly and gave her knee a squeeze.

"Hey!" she said, squirming a little with my squeeze, tickled. She batted at my hand but not hard enough to indicate that she wanted me to stop touching her. "No, they aren't going to kick me out. I'm barely an important part of the guild. It's just for fun, you know?" I could feel my heart quickening at our little flirtations. I didn't want to remove my hand from her leg for anything. It felt so right.

"Well, okay," I said. "Maybe we could hang out, order in for dinner, watch a movie. How does that sound?"

"Awesome," said Henry. "That sounds like a chill Saturday night."

I could feel a bit of courage building up inside of me, like a balloon had been slowly inflating in my heart and I didn't begin to realize it until it had grown large and noticeable. Maybe it was Henry's laugh when I squeezed her knee, her playful smack of my hand, the lightness on her cute, pale face. Or maybe it was how close we sat together on the couch, the implication that we'd spend the evening together, or her willingness to forgo her usual rituals to spend time with me. Whatever it was, it was palpable. I knew she felt it too. I could see it in those steel blue-grey eyes.

Before I knew it, I felt myself leaning in slowly towards Henry, my hand firm against her knee, my other arm draped over the back of the couch. As I closed in on her, I could see Henry take a deep breath, a bit of rosiness build in her cheeks, her eyes wide with anticipation and excitement. Her bottom lip hung just slightly off of her top lip and once my face approached hers our lips tenderly met, kindling a soft and sweet kiss, a kiss I had been eager to consummate since I first saw her standing there in my office. I closed my eyes and melted into her, moaning out a gentle little whimper as I felt Henry's warm hand press down against my own.

I could feel my anxiety dissolve as we kissed, my fears and worries dissipating. In that moment, it was only us. I didn't think about what day it was or the time, I didn't think about that work text lingering on my phone, and I didn't think of my build up of problems and woes. No, I could only meditate on kissing Henry, on savoring this fleeting moment, of enjoying the joining of our wet lips, feeling the desire in my heart and the butterflies in my belly flitting along with this romantic novelty. I felt light.

After moment, both Henry and I pulled back from one another, opened our eyes, and smiled. She giggled bashfully, girlishly, and I took a deep breath to still my thumping heart.

"So... Thai?" she said with a smile, lightening the mood up a bit from the romance I knew we both felt.

"Definitely," I said. I gazed deeply into Henry's eyes, looking through the lenses hovering over them, catching myself just slightly in the reflection. She was kind, endearing, adorable, and I felt undeniably smitten.

LATER ON THAT EVENING, with empty containers of take out strewn about on the coffee table in front of us, a movie playing on the television across the room, Henry and I sat together on the couch, cuddled close under a blanket, making out with one another with lust in the air. I had slipped into some casual lounge pants and a tank top, Henry dressed down to just her leggings and white ribbed tank, our bodies warmly enmeshed with each other and the blanket, kissing with soft, wet, smacking sounds.

I felt Henry's hand press against my chest, tenderly massaging my breast, giving it a firm squeeze as our lips intertwined. I couldn't help myself as I moaned into her mouth, enthralled by her loving touch, arching my back to allow her greater access to my chest, braless under my thin tank top. Eager from her petting, I slipped my fingers under the back of her shirt, touching her bare skin now with my hands, flesh on flesh, then lowering them down to fiddle with the waistband of her leggings. I pulled it away from her skin with my thumbs, sinking them down into her leggings while my fingers remained outside, feeling then the thin fabric of her panties underneath.

"Mmm," said Henry, moving away from our kiss, cheek to cheek now, her lips hovering near my ear. "I like feeling you touch my back."

"Your skin is warm," I cooed, kissing her then on the side of the head, my face bumping into the arm of her glasses. With her approval, I let my fingers drop into the back of her leggings, fingertips rubbing against the elastic band of her panties.

"This is so much better than gaming," said Henry absentmindedly, craning her neck to the side, to which I eagerly dropped my face and began kissing it. She moaned as I kissed the tenderness of her neck and then she thoughtfully moved her long, brown hair out of the way of my attentions.

"I'm glad you think so," I said between kisses. "Have you ever had sex in the game?" I asked, feeling a bit lusty and adventurous, kissing Henry's neck, slowly easing my fingers into the back of her panties.

"Mm hmm," she affirmed, her eyes closed, neck shifted, a smile on her lips.

"How does that work?"

"We open a chat window," said Henry, softly sighing with my kisses. "And we talk sexy to each other there. It was our characters having sex."

"And that can get you hot?" I asked, interested in her experience.

"Oh yeah," she said. "My friend who I do it with is a good writer. Mmm. She writes erotica."

"Maybe I've read some of her stuff," I said, and then laughed nervously as I considered what I was admitting to Henry.

"Help me out of these leggings," said Henry innocently. I grinned at her and with my fingers already threaded into the rear of her leggings, I helped slide them off over her ass while Henry took care of moving the front down. Together we moved the fabric down her thighs until they hung at her feet, Henry using her feet together to push out of them. She now laid there next to me, under the blanket, in just her panties and tank.

We returned to kissing one another and feeling eager to go exploring, I pushed my hand between her thighs and began to caress her mound over top of her panties, feeling the subtle wetness of her pussy slip through the fabric, along with feeling the little tickle of coarse hairs piercing through the material, lightly prickling my fingers.

"Oh jeez," Henry moaned, squirming slightly as she enjoyed my touch. She widened her legs slightly, inviting me in, her hand slipping up and holding me by the side of the face as we kissed.

"You're wet," I murmured. "It's nice."

"Mmm," she said, wiggling her body. "That made me even wetter."

Giving her lips a tender squeeze through her panties, I sensually pushed my mouth against hers once more and began another long, lusty kiss, the bare skin of our arms and shoulders lightly sticking together as our bodies touched, our long hair falling down over our faces, tickling, as the movie displayed on the TV flickered light and sound in our direction.

"I like making out with you," said Henry between kisses as her hands ran all over my upper half.

"You don't think we're moving too fast, do you?" I asked with caution, definitely not interested in stopping but careful to go at Henry's pace.

"No," she said matter-of-factly, pulling back from me for a moment to remove her glasses and fling them onto the coffee table. She smiled lustily at me, her steel blue eyes looking into mine, twinkling with desire. Her eyes had a bit of a sleepy, droopy look to them as the eyes of many full-time glasses wearers had. And that look, indolent, relaxed, casual, got my blood pulsing at an even greater clip through my heated body.

"I just don't want you to think I'm taking advantage of you," I said, kissing, petting, fondling. "You know, the whole work thing."

"Who's to say I'm not taking advantage of you?" she posited with coyness. "Hey, you want to see something?"

"Okay," I agreed, our kiss slowly ended, our bodies shifting back from one another momentarily.

With a conspiratorial grin across her lips, Henry reached underneath her tank top in the back and deftly unfastened her bra. She then grabbed her tank by the bottom and lifted it up above her head, pulling her bra off with it, balling up these articles of clothing and letting them drop to the floor. Arching her back, she foisted her chest out toward me, displaying her breasts, medium-sized, rounded, firm, yet seemingly weightless as they hung, and through each of her nipples I saw a silver barbell. Henry had pierced nipples.

"Do you like them?" she said, looking down at her own chest, taking up one of her breasts and gazing at the piercing. "I had them done a couple months ago."

"Would you think I was a total weirdo square if I told you I'd never been with a girl who had her nipples pierced?" I asked sheepishly. This caused Henry to giggle.

"No, of course not," she comforted. "What do you think? You can touch."

I slowly moved my hand forward until my fingertips reached her chest. I felt her nipple, I felt the barbell going through it, the little bulbs on each end, and I could see the excitement growing over her face as she watched me touch her.

"Mmm," she sighed as my finger ran over her piercing. "It makes the hair on the back of my neck stand up."

"You're so beautiful," I mused, still petting her pierced

nipple. Henry remained in her presented state, happy that I too enjoyed her piercings.

"I'm getting cold now," she said, wiggling her chest slightly at me. "Maybe we could go get under the blankets in your bed?"

"Let's," I said, planting a slow, soft, sweet kiss on her lips. We then stood up together from the couch, Henry wearing only a thin little pair of pale pink panties, slightly loose at the bottom of her ass, her pierced breasts swaying with her moves. As she leaned over to pick her glasses up from the coffee table, her tits hung downward, pointing toward the floor. I picked up the TV remote and switched it off, though my eyes remained on her.

Henry trotted away from the couch, still a bit unfamiliar with my condo. She looked back and forth as we traipsed out of the living room, walking by the kitchen, and we made our way toward the hall that lead to my bedroom.

HENRY ENTERED MY BEDROOM FIRST, the room fully dark as we walked in, but I could tell by how eager she was to make her way toward my bed that she was ready to be passionate. I was beaming as I watched her body bounce, feeling so joyous that she liked me, so hungry for I knew what we were about to do together. I flipped on the secondary light switch in my room, causing a couple low, orange lamps to come to life and give my bedroom a sultry, sexy atmosphere.

Her overall demeanor had started out somewhat nerdy and bashful, but as our night went on, from the fun and social brunch, to the ice skating, to ordering take out and then our little make out session on the couch, Henry's enthusiasm and comfort had grown exponentially. And now here she was, lounging only in her diminutive pink panties, climbing up onto my bed, her butt bouncing down onto the comforter, her body writhing in alluring, seductive movements. She held her glasses for a moment in her hand, before languidly reaching over, her swollen chest calling to me, and setting her frames lightly onto my bedside table.

"Come over here," Henry half-whined at me, smiling, her legs kicking a bit back and forth. "And get undressed like me."

I followed her command, stepping further into the room, untying my lounge pants and letting them fall to my ankles. Underneath I had made sure to put on some nice panties when I changed earlier, wearing a dark purple thong now, and I slinked toward the bed. Next I lifted my tank off my torso, flipping it away as I removed it from my head, revealing my chest for Henry to see. She watched me with a curious smile, an inviting smile, and I mounted the bed and crawled in her direction.

We collided into one another once again, warm skin melting together, arms wrapping around, lips meeting. I was overjoyed by this arousing cupidity, letting my hands do the talking for me as I explored along Henry's torso, her chest and pierced nipples, and even moving a hand between her legs to grope at her womanhood through the attenuate material of her panties. I laid half on top of her, half to her side, the two of us lustily searching each other with nimble fingers, our lips hotly and moistly pushing together.

I felt Henry's hand move down my backside, graze over the thin waistband of my panties, and plug a single finger into the string of my thong. She moved her finger downward, causing the string to lift out from my crack, and she just simply moved her finger slowly up and down along the stretchiness of the string as we fervently kissed.

"I'm crazy about you," I sighed between kisses, instantly feeling self-conscious by my impulsive pillow talk. But Henry just giggled and cooed, rubbing her body into mine, our chests pushed together, our joint arousal growing.

"Hey Netty," she murmured, removing her finger from my thong string and gently placing her hands on my sides. "I've got a secret for you."

"Yeah?" I said, leaning down and kissing her neck tenderly.

"I'm really good at going down here," she said, on the word "here" her fingers slithered between my legs and gave me a light pinch through the fabric of my underwear. "Will you let me?"

"I would love that," I said, pulling away from her and rolling over onto my back. Henry eagerly leapt up from her laying position, sitting next to me on her knees, her hands making their way to the elastic band of my thong.

"Let me take these off," she said, taking hold of my underwear and beginning to slip them off my hips. Henry slowly pulled the small article of clothing down my thighs and then off my feet, giving them an absentminded toss as she returned her attention to my body.

"I'm a little prickly down here," I said, running my fingers through my own bush. I had long been in the habit of shaving myself completely, despite my lack of romance as of late, but my fur had grown out a bit over the past week or so and I was worried that I was a bit too bristly between my thighs.

"That's okay," said Henry with a grin. She slipped her fingers into her own panties and tilted the front forward to reveal her pubic hair, bushy and full. "I just edge mine and keep the rest as nature intended." I laughed softly, reaching my hand out and running my fingers through her brown fur. I could feel some of her hair wetly matted down from when I had fondled her through her panties earlier.

"All right," I said, feeling a chill run up my back, wrapping my arms around myself and hugging. "Show me what you've got." My comfort level was increasing with Henry. I felt relaxed with her, open, knowing that she would accept most anything I threw at her. It was her own comfort with herself that inspired a similar comfort in me. Henry nodded energetically at my proposal and climbed around me, positioning herself between my legs as I widened myself to let her have her way.

I felt her palm beginning to massage over my pussy mound, gliding up and down. The ball of her hand rubbed against my moistening lips and slipped upwards along my slit, her fingertips moving over my short fur. I sighed contently and gripped myself tighter in an embrace.

"You have a beautiful pussy," Henry ruminated aloud, still gingerly massaging me with her warm hand. "Your little labia peeking out from your lips just so." As she said this, her fingers gave my inner labia a soft squeeze and a tug. I felt positively spongey between my legs, wet from Henry's attention, and blowing up on the inside with feelings of intense longing.

"Ooh," I softly moaned at Henry's touch. She traced a single finger over my moistened slit, sliding up and down along it, tenderly parting my lips with the length of her finger and gently fondling me. I couldn't help but close my eyes, a marching band going off inside my head with how great my arousal was getting. It had been too long since I had sexual attention like this and I was positively bursting with yearning for Henry. She drove me wild in all her geeky glory.

"So pretty," she cooed at me. Then I felt a sudden rush of warmth, Henry's face moving in close to me, her finger still manipulating my aching lips. I cried out an excited groan as I felt her mouth wetly push up against my pussy lips, her tongue sneak out and give me a slow lick, and then plant a sweet kiss on my clit. The anticipation for this moment had been intense and, as it came to fruition, I felt almost as though I could climax right then and there. I certainly had some pent up sexual aggressions that desperately needed to be released.

Henry's mouth settled on top of my clit, slurping at my wetness, offering me tender little sucks. Her finger continued to indolently fondle me, coaxing my pussy to become creamy with excitement, and then finally she pressed against me with a firm motion, parted my lips around her finger, and entered me with ease.

"Oh God," I groaned, my ass twisting slightly against the sheets below. My inner thighs had grown humid and sweaty, my heart raced, my breathing was growing laborious. I could feel Henry's methodical licks at my clit, interspersed with tender sucking. The panting sounds coming from my own gaping mouth were punctuated by the sporadic slurps and suckles of Henry attending to my moistness.

Henry paused for a breath, letting her cheek rest against my lower stomach and just watch, her penetrating finger sliding out of me and deftly moving up and down through my slit until it settled on my clit, giving me quick little circle rubs and sending my head swimming.

I opened my eyes for a moment and looked down the length of my naked body at her and I reached out, running my fingers through her soft brown tendrils, letting her hair move through the spaces between my fingers, lovingly petting her as I enjoyed her sensual assiduity. She was wonderful. So cute and caring, so pretty and puckish, so geeky and gleeful. Although I wanted to continue watching, I once more felt Henry's lips meet with my clit and I dropped my head back to the pillows with a pleasured moan, tightly closing my eyes, and widening my legs further for her in exhilaration.

As the pleasure mounted, my hips started to slowly lift up off the bed and then fall back down, Henry's head moving along with me. She kept one hand on my side, the other penetrating me with a single gliding finger, and her mouth aligned to my clit. I felt fuzzy, dizzy, drunk, a tickle growing in my midsection. I felt my lower half compress and release, squeeze and relax. Although I was definitely moaning, it was like my ears had gone deaf for a moment as my hips thrust upwards and my body clenched. None of this deterred Henry, however, as her attention was steady and true.

"Oh yeah," I exclaimed, my fingers threaded into Henry's hair, giving her a bit of a tug. The floodgates opened and my pleasure came spilling out. I could see little twinkles behind my eyelids, almost as though someone had knocked me over the head with a plank of wood, giddy and groggy and bewildered, unable to control the various squirms and wiggles of my climaxing body. "I'm coming," I murmured out reflexively as my body swiftly shifted to one side and then the other. I heard the subtle softness of a laugh come from between my legs.

I wriggled through my orgasm and Henry lifted her head up from my lower half, eyes up at me, watching me as I came, her wet fingers gently petting my pussy lips in a tender and loving gesture. The smile on her face indicated her happiness at how well she had driven me to this summit of passion.

Once my body slowed in its automatic, writhing motions, Henry slithered up the length of me and laid down against me, our flesh mingling, her hand remaining on my pussy and continuing to stroke me. With each caress, I felt a shockwave course through me and I giggled with delight, softening into that familiar post-coital daze. I wrapped an arm around Henry and pulled her close.

"You weren't kidding," I whispered, my chest heaving up and down as I tried to steady my breath. "Oh my God, that was just... amazing."

"You tasted really good," said Henry, licking her lips and wiping at her mouth a bit with the back of her hand. "Botanical, really." I laughed at her description.

"Botanical?" I repeated. "I don't think anybody has ever called my pussy botanical before."

"Well, it is," she cooed, giving me another delicate rub with her soaked fingers. I squirmed and squeaked.

"I want to taste you," I said, my fingers prying at her little pink panties, eager to please her now with a revitalized sense of purpose.

"Let's cuddle for a moment," said Henry, burrowing against me contentedly with a sweet sigh. I was so happy to be lying there in bed with her. I never wanted our lovemaking to end.

As we relaxed there together, our breathing becoming syncopated, a gentle sense of calm washing over the two of us, Henry rolled away from me slightly and moved her hands down along her body until she reached the band of her underwear. She shimmied them over her butt, down her thighs, and then kicked them off her feet. I couldn't help but watch intently as she got naked. With a grin on her face, turning toward me slightly, one hand placed on her own bush and petting herself, she spoke up in a lusty whisper.

"Okay Netty," she said. "Your turn."

Monday at work I couldn't think straight. My mind was focused only on Henry. I was blown over, infatuated, near obsessed with her. I even thought for a moment that I could call up our IT firm with a fake problem and request her to come over and visit me. Of course, I knew it would have been one of our usual consultants who'd come by, but in my daydream it would be Henry and we'd close my office door and make love right there on my desk.

Although I spent much of the day staring at my spreadsheets, clicking through the client database, shuffling papers around, I couldn't really keep my attention on my various tasks. It only made my work pile up higher. That text I had received on Saturday when I was with Henry was about a potential new client, a very large pension fund that was looking to invest with our approach. It was exciting and important, something that could make our company a lot of money. I mean, when you take 1% in expenses from a billion dollar fund, you do pretty well. But I just couldn't get my mind off of my encounter with Henry. I felt my heart rate increase just thinking about her.

With my head in my hands, elbows propped on my desk, blankly staring into the screen, my coworker Kate slipped undetected into my office. I didn't notice her until she gently knocked on the metal doorframe.

"Hey Netty," she said. "You awake?"

"What?" I said, shaking my head and then looking past my screen and seeing her. "Oh. Kate. I'm sorry. What's up?"

"Are you okay?" she asked, coming further into my office and bracing herself against one of my guest chairs. "You've been off in the clouds all day."

"I'm all right," I said, trying to be reassuring. "Just a long weekend."

"Tell me about it," said Kate, shaking her head and widening her eyes in familiarity. "Sunday brunch turned into an all day bender for me," she joked. "By the time I stumbled into bed Sunday night, my head was spinning as my husband totally railed me. I mean, I was so close to passing out with him still inside me."

"TMI, Kate," I said, feeling a grin build on my face. Kate was funny and I enjoyed her company at work.

"Sorry," she said with a laugh. "I'm just reminiscing out loud." She looked down to her watch and hummed a bit. "It's near quitting time, want to go get a glass of wine or something? I could use it after nursing this hangover all day."

"No," I said softly. "I'm trying to, um, abstain."

"Abstain?" she said almost incredulously. "Good luck. With this new pension account coming in soon, I'm going to be under too much pressure. Need my wine!"

"Yeah," I mused defeatedly.

"Well, get your shit together," said Kate finally, getting to the point of her visit. "Everyone's been like, 'what's up with Netty?' today and you need to turn it around," she said.

"We're relying on you to lead the presentation for our department."

"I know," I said. "I'm just kind of..." I said, trailing off. I looked past Kate to make sure nobody else was milling around outside of my office. "Lovestruck."

"Oh stop!" said Kate with an animated face. "You found a little slit to lick?" She grinned at her lesbian joke.

"You're lucky that we're so close," I said. "Don't say that to any lesbian you just met." Her laughter bordered on cackling as she got a rise out of her own perceived hilarity.

"Don't worry about me, Netty," she said. "I stopped caring about being offensive a long time ago."

"Will you close my door?" I asked. "I just don't want anybody to hear about this."

"Okay," she said, nodding, her face scrunching like she inferred something was wrong. She walked in her heels over to the door and shut it, then turning and walking back toward my desk and taking a seat in front of me. "Spill your guts."

"I did find a slit to lick," I said, trying to stifle my smile. "This chick is driving me bonkers. I can't stop thinking about her."

"That's awesome!" said Kate. "I'm so happy for you. It's been too long since you were involved with someone. What's she like?"

"So that's where it gets a little troublesome," I said. "This girl — I mean, this young woman — is kind of related to our company in a way."

"Nasty," she said with a devilish smirk. "You're bad, Netty."

"No, I'm serious," I said. "She's, well, part of our IT team."

"Oh my God!" she exclaimed, bringing her hand up to her mouth and gasping. "She's a geek!"

"Yeah, sorta," I said. "I'm less concerned about that and more concerned about the whole conflict of interest thing. You know, dating one of our contractors?"

"Oh yeah," said Kate, leaning back in the chair. "Yeah, that's bad. But I mean, this is the girl who was in here last Friday night?" she asked. "Mousy brown hair, big black glasses."

"Yeah, that's her," I said.

"Netty," said Kate, leveling with me. "That girl's a nerd. You're a pretty young woman with a job in finance who attended an Ivy League school and was in one of the most exclusive sororities on campus," she said, smiling like I was nuts. "I know it's silly to take all that college bullshit with you into the real world, but well, it sort of does translate to the real world."

I felt myself getting a little upset by Kate. She had always struck me as a good friend at work, someone who reminded me of my friends from the past, someone who could make me laugh like I used to. But as she continued to speak, all of these positives I had felt slowly began to morph into negatives.

"Have you tried meeting someone through a professional mixer?" Kate continued on, an almost pitying look on her face. "Maybe you could meet someone further along in their career like yourself."

"This isn't why I brought this up to you, Kate," I said, feeling myself shake a little bit with adrenaline. Here I was, finally feeling happy and positive about a relationship, and Kate was trying to bring me down. "I'm worried about the implications. The conflict of interest," I said. "I like how geeky this girl is."

"Really?" she said incredulously. "C'mon Netty." She just couldn't let it go. I knew there was no use fighting it. The more I thought about it, the more I realized that people like Kate were the exact type of people I was trying to get away from. Snarky, negative, judgmental. And it was people like Henry, people who were comfortable with themselves, accepting, unflappable, that I was really beginning to gravitate towards.

"Just follow me for a second," I said. "Do you think this would cause a problem at work? The fact that she's a contractor we hire?"

"Well," said Kate, averting her eyes, tilting her head. "I mean, yeah, I could see it being an issue. What if the relationship goes south and you've got to see her at work?"

"True," I admitted.

"Or, like, she gets pissed at you for some reason and screws with our computers," continued Kate. "Yeah, it's probably not an advisable thing."

"Should I talk to Levi about it?" I asked with caution.

"Oh my God, no," said Kate. "Do you think Levi wants to be bothered by something like this? I mean, first, he'd say not to do it. And second, he'd probably give you shit for talking about something other than the financial markets."

"All right," I said solemnly. "Maybe I'll talk to Trevor."

"He would be the one to talk to," said Kate. "He's COO after all. But still, I wouldn't even bring it up with him. I think your best bet is to just forget about this and find someone else." Kate pushed the chair back and stood up, indicating our conversation was over. "Classic conflict of interest. Plus, Netty, you know you could find some ultra girly lipstick lesbian who's more in tune with your lifestyle."

"I guess," I said.

"Get your focus back," she said and meandered toward the door. She opened the door a crack and turned back to look at me. "It's going to be a busy week."

And with that, Kate slipped out of my office. My heart had sunk. She had only increased my worry about escalating things with Henry. I could feel my anxiety levels growing by the second.

Henry and I texted throughout the week but we didn't see each other. I was worried about what the outcome would be if we continued our tryst, but I had yet to confide that in her. My plan was to avoid face-to-face contact with her for a couple days while I figured it all out in my head. And it didn't help that I was completely buried at work with preparation for the new account. Henry was sweet and empathetic about my stressful work life, not in the least bit worried it seemed that we couldn't make plans to get together that week. Meanwhile, I was torn up inside.

Kate's little speech about Henry being a geek and not being right for me really brought me down. I know it was completely unfounded and I know it was against my feelings, but I couldn't help but let it upset me. It made me want to crack open a bottle of wine and chug the entire thing. I actually thought about doing that for a split second, it was certainly tempting, though I knew I'd be better off if I just left the booze on the shelf.

Another Friday evening was upon me, my brain feeling absolutely fried from the hectic workweek, and I was trying to finish up the layout on a PDF so I could send it to operations for approval. As my eyes began to cross from looking too deeply into the monitor, my phone started to buzz on my desk. Looking down, I noticed a text from Henry.

"Hey," she texted. "Movie tonight?"

"Still working," I typed back. "Don't you have your game?"

"I want to see you," she typed. "Game can wait."

I gazed down at my phone, my heart heavy, wanting so badly to see her but afraid of what the outcome would be. As I contemplated what I could write back to her, I felt a presence lingering in my door. I looked up and spotted Trevor, a smarmy-looking playboy type, expensive striped button-down shirt, his hair receding but slicked back. He was our COO, responsible for keeping all the parts of the organization moving, lead on all dealings with clients and investors, and the kind of guy who seems really cool at first but a bit of a creep the more you get to know him.

"Netty," he said casually, leaning against the doorframe. In his hand was a martini. Fridays after 5PM was always cocktail hour in the office, which was mostly taken advantage of by the people who weren't responsible for all the heavy lifting. He hoisted his glass at me and smiled. "Can I make you a vodka martini?"

"No thanks," I said. "I'm still working on this PDF."

Trevor slinked into my office, his grin dripping off the sides of his face. I knew he had a thing for me, and even though Trevor certainly knew I was a lesbian, he persisted with laying on the charm whenever he had me alone. He brought the martini to his lips and took a small sip as he neared my desk. Then he sat on the edge of my desk, one leg on the floor and the other hanging off.

"Staying late?" he asked.

"I'm hoping not," I said. "I'm almost finished here." I tried to avoid eye contact with him, opting to instead focus on my screen and at least pretend like I was getting work done.

My phone buzzed once more and I looked down at it, seeing that Henry had texted again. I didn't reach for it to check the message, however, instead keeping focus on my screen to see if I could get rid of Trevor.

"Annette," said Trevor, adjusting himself there on the edge of my desk. "I'm here to talk to you about this thing you've got going on."

"What thing?" I asked, looking up to him, probably appearing like a deer in headlights. "This presentation?"

"This thing," he continued. "With someone from our IT contractors."

I took a deep breath and pushed my mouse away. My eyes moved from my screen to meet with Trevor's.

"I don't like to pry in the personal lives of employees," he said, swishing his drink around in the glass. "But it's not very appropriate to get involved with one of our contractors. It could cause problems down the line."

"I understand," I said. "How did you hear about this?"

"Word gets around," he said. "I run this office and I've got a good grasp of what's going on." He sipped his martini.

"Things are very discreet," I said. "You don't have to worry about me."

"See to that," said Trevor. "You're close to making partner here, Netty. Another couple of years and you could be an owner with the rest of us. You don't want to screw that up."

"I agree," I said.

"Let's just keep this all between us," he said, standing up from my desk and straightening himself out. "We don't need to get HR or anyone else involved with this. Just exercise caution and don't do something unadvised if you value your position here."

"Got it, Trevor," I said with a forced smile. "Anything else?"

"A drink?" he asked again, showing me his glass.

"I can't," I said, motioning my head toward my monitor. "Work to do."

"Suit yourself," he said. "Evening." Trevor turned from me and made his way out of my office, ambling through the cubicles of some of the other client service employees, all of which who had already gone home. It was dark outside the office windows, one of those oh so lovely perks of winter, and the skyscrapers of Chicago's downtown Loop had become ablaze with little lights in little offices filled with little people like me, still working on a Friday night.

Once Trevor was out of sight, I quickly grabbed my phone and unlocked it to read Henry's message.

"So…?" was Henry's message, written there in my text message app.

"Not sure yet," I typed back. "Can I text you in a bit?"

"Sure."

I sighed and set my phone back down. The clock on my computer told me it was nearing 6PM. I shook my head and returned to my work.

WALKING DOWN MY SNOWY STREET, I tightened my coat around myself and clung to my leather bag, increasing the speed of my gait as I drew closer to my building. It was dark and cold out and I was eager to get into the warmth of my condo. As I approached the door to my building, however, I saw somebody standing there near the entrance, bundled up in a black wool coat and a white fluffy hat, a backpack on their back. The person turned to me and as soon as I saw the black frames on her face I knew it was Henry. I almost stumbled when I saw her.

"Henry," I said in surprise when I came upon her. "What are you doing here?"

"Waiting for you," she said. "I just wanted to see you and I thought I'd stop by. Why didn't you text me back?"

"Oh shit," I said, looking down and shaking my head. "I'm sorry. I'm just totally fried. Work is killing me."

"Can we step inside?" she asked. "I'm freezing out here."

"Yes!" I said. "Of course." I moved past her and pushed my key fob against the door sensor, opening it up so both Henry and I could walk through into my building's entryway. There was another glass door to go through once inside and as we got through that, the warmth of the indoors finally hit us. The sudden change in temperature caused Henry's glasses to fog up and she grinned at me, showing it off.

"Foggy," she said, removing her frames and wiping the fog from them with her gloves.

I smiled and reached out to touch her arm tenderly.

"I'm really sorry," I said again. "I didn't mean to leave you hanging. I've just got a lot on my mind."

"So do you want to hang out tonight?" she asked, pushing her glasses back onto her face. "Or should I just go back out into the cold?"

"Well, when you put it that way," I said teasingly. "I guess I really don't have a choice, do I?"

"Let me come up!" she mock demanded, stomping a foot to hammer her joke home.

"I guess you can come up," I said coquettishly, turning from Henry and beginning to walk toward the elevator. I felt a little torn, unsure what this would all lead to. I wanted to be with her but I was worried.

"Wait for me!" she exclaimed, scurrying after me.

We removed our winter gear together in the foyer of my condo, hanging up coats, slipping out of boots and setting them on the mat to dry, pulling off gloves and scarves and all that. Henry set her backpack down near the door. Although I had a pit of anxiety building up inside of me from all the negativity I'd been feeling at work, seeing Henry made it all almost dissolve. Almost. Although my passions were cranked up by just being near her, the logic in my brain was trying to figure out what my body was doing.

Henry scooted in further to my condo wearing dark green surplus-style pants, tight against her legs and tucked into some heavy-weight wool socks, a white button-down blouse splattered with colorful floral prints up top, and she kept her winter cap on her head. I felt so drained from my day, even as I watched how animated Henry was, and I craved a glass of wine. But I had gotten rid of all the alcohol in my condo, so I simply resolved to let that craving pass.

"Did you have a good day at work?" I asked her, following her toward the living room.

"Yeah, fine," she said. "I was at my office all day just doing remote stuff. I love the days when I don't have to leave the office to go to a client. It's far too cold out anyway to be running around the city."

As Henry eased herself down onto my couch, I continued on through my condo and into the kitchen to put a kettle of water on for tea, taking out cups and teabags for the two of us.

"Honey?" I called out to her.

"Please!"

Armed with our mugs, steaming with the hot water, I moved back into the living room and put our tea down on the coffee table. Henry beamed up at me, her glasses halfway down her nose. I smiled at her with a bit of pain.

"Is everything okay?" Henry asked me, her face changing to mirror mine.

"Henry," I said softly, sitting down next to her, our legs touching. I gently placed my palm on her thigh.

"Oh no," she said. "I've been in this situation before." She slid away from me slightly and had a defensive look in her eye. "You're going to end this, aren't you?"

"I just—" I said, searching my brain for my words. But I felt so strained that it was difficult to figure out what I was trying to communicate. I didn't even know where I was going with this. "I like you, Henry. I'm crazy about you. But—"

"But..." she said, interrupting me, raising her brow.

"I'm worried," I said. "I'm worried about work and how

this," I said, motioning back and forth between us. "Affects our relationship at work."

"But I barely even work with you," said Henry, her body still standoffish. "I mean, I'm at your office once every six months, sometimes not even that, and it's pretty much always at night or on a weekend."

"I mentioned you to one of my coworkers," I said. "And then word got around to my boss, who told me that it was pretty much a bad idea for both our companies if you and I were to get involved."

"I don't believe it," she said. Her voice cracked slightly and I could see her eyes growing watery behind her glasses. "I don't even get a chance?"

"I don't want it to be this way," I mourned.

"So why did you even invite me up?" she asked. "If you were just gonna dump me?"

I didn't know what to say. Obviously I was of two minds. The words that had been coming out of my mouth seemed distant, like they were being spoken by someone else. Me, my voice, Annette, she wanted to spend the night with Henry and laugh and kiss and be joyful. But this other voice, this unfamiliar voice of responsibility, of guilt, this voice was the one who so suddenly seemed to be in charge of my words.

After a moment of silence, Henry hoisted herself up off the couch and began walking across the room and toward the door.

"Wait!" I exclaimed. She stopped there in her socks, pivoting, looking at me. "Henry, I—"

"No, it's best if I go now," she said. "I'm still cold from outside so it won't be a big adjustment." She moseyed over to her boots and began to slip into them.

"Stay," I murmured.

"What?"

"Stay," I repeated, a little louder this time.

"Grr," Henry growled. "So which is it?"

"I just want to talk," I said sheepishly. "I want to talk through this."

Henry stood there wearing just one boot. After a moment of silence between the two of us she stepped out of her boot and wandered back over to me, her big wool socks stuck to the floor as she moved. Reaching the coffee table, she stood there, arms crossed, unhappy visage on her face.

"So," she said. "Talk."

"I'm still trying to work this all through in my head," I said. "There's so much going on in there and I'm confused."

"I don't know about you," said Henry in a huff. "Maybe you're a little more promiscuous than me, but I don't just fuck somebody on a lark. I had fun with you last Saturday and it all seemed so real and that's why I got intimate. If I'd known this was just some thing, I never would have done that."

"It's not like that at all," I said. "Oh, I could really use a glass of wine."

"Well, Netty, it sure seems like it's like that," she said. "I'm really hurt," said Henry, pushing a finger up under her glasses to wipe at a tear. "I've been thinking about you all week, looking forward to seeing you."

"I've been thinking about you all week, too!" I said. "I haven't been able to get anything done, I've been so torn up about this."

"So what are we doing?" she asked. "Why are you making me cry like this?"

"I'm crazy about you," I said once again, sullenly, shaking my head. "I don't want it to be like this."

"It doesn't have to be," she said, "It can be however we want."

Henry could see the sadness on my face and her own face softened. Without another word, she wound around the coffee table and lowered herself back onto the couch, snuggling up next to me. I wrapped my arm around her shoulders and her arms threaded around my waist.

"I'm just in a weird place right now," I said. "This stopping drinking thing, insanity at work." I felt a tear run out of my eye as we embraced each other. "I didn't mean to start it like this."

"I know," said Henry softly.

"I'm changing," I said. "I don't know what's up with me lately, but I'm changing. Something's happening."

"What is it?" she asked.

"It's like I'm becoming a different person somehow," I said. "Like I'm shedding the skin of an old Netty and emerging as something different, a different mind. I don't know how else to describe it. It's silly," I said, looking away.

"Can we get comfortable?" said Henry sweetly. "Can we get comfortable, order some food — mediterranean maybe? — huddle under a blanket and watch a movie?" Henry brought her hand up and slowly stroked my arm, her head leaning into my shoulder.

"I would definitely like that," I said, kissing her gently on the head, feeling a few thin strands of her hair stick to my lips as I pulled away.

LIKE THE WEEKEND PREVIOUS, after our little dinner and movie date, Henry and I ended up in my bed, both of us totally bare, rolling around with each other, giggling, pinching, kissing. I was so happy with her, so joyful, she made me feel young. I mean, I know I'm not that old or anything, but after thirty something changes and you just start to feel like an adult. Being with Henry, I felt like I was right back in college or something, exploring other girls for the first time, reveling in the novelty and excitement of caressing the soft body of another woman.

The lights were dim in my bedroom and I had put on some low music, something a bit dance-y but steady and calm. I sat on top of Henry, who grinned up at me, still wearing her glasses, the little steel barbells through her nipples glistening in the faint light. Spreading my hands out, I eased my palms against her skin, over her sides, and slowly moved my hands upwards until I met her breasts in the crook of my hands between my thumbs and forefingers. Feeling the passion build up inside of me, I gave Henry's tits an arduous squeeze.

"Ooh!" she squeaked, wiggling under me. "Mmm, do it again."

So I did. I squeezed her breasts firmer this time, moving my palms upwards on them until my thumbs reached her nipples, giving them both a swift circular rub, feeling the piercings on my fingertips.

"Oh Netty," she cooed. "That's nice."

"I want to taste you," I lustily intoned, leaning my face down and leaving a sweet kiss on her lips. Righting myself again, I moved a hand to her face and gently pulled her glasses off.

"I can't wait," said Henry, giddiness and excitement punctuating her face. I leaned over, stretching my nude body away from her though remaining in my straddling position, and placed her glasses on the bedside table. "Did you see what I did?"

"Mmm? What's that?" I asked with a mellifluous smile. I felt like I was in a different world from my own when I was with Henry. Like some other universe in which only we existed.

"I must have got into bed too quickly and you missed it," she said with an impish grin. "Feel me down there," said Henry, pointing down between her legs.

Reaching my hand under myself where I straddled her, I eased my fingers into the crevice between Henry's thighs and felt. Her skin was soft, supple, elastic. Moving my hand further down, I felt her lips, her moistened slit, her warmth.

"You shaved it all off?" I asked with a laugh. "Why? I liked your fur."

"I dunno," she grinned and shrugged against the pillows. "I thought it would be fun to do. I haven't done it in a long time."

"I should have done mine," I said absentmindedly, looking down at my own mound, my hair having grown out even more since the previous time we were together.

"I don't mind," said Henry, snaking her hand between my legs and plucking her fingers through my fur. "I like you anyway you come."

"Why do you like me?" I said songfully. "Don't you think I'm crazy?"

"Well, for starters," said Henry, counting on her fingers. "You're, like, really pretty."

"Stop!" I said, blushing. "C'mon."

"You're like a 10 compared to me being, I dunno, like a 6," she said, somewhat bashfully. "On the looks scale."

"You're insane," I said, giving one of her nipples a tweak and inciting a giggle out of her. "There's no way I'm a 10 and you're way higher than a 6."

"Okay, so, you're smart," she said, continuing her finger count. "You're not just some airhead. You can hold a conversation."

"I did go to an Ivy League school," I said with faux humility. "They don't let just anyone in."

"Right," she said, smacking my thigh. I grinded down on top of her, feeling myself glide over her own smoothness. "That's nice," she said, squirming into it, resting her hands on my thighs now.

"Go on," I said. "Why else do you like me? I still don't get it."

"I dunno," said Henry, looking off. I could tell she was growing a bit serious. "I guess, well, I like you because you see me. A lot of people don't seem to see me. I'm kinda geeky, if you didn't catch on."

"I love that you're geeky," I said. "It's a breath of fresh air."

"Yeah?" she said, her seriousness melting into delight.

"Yeah," I affirmed. "I like you because you're real. You don't put on a show. You're just you, you're cool with that, and screw everybody else." I smiled down at her, feeling a closeness to her more than just purely physical. Though that was really nice, too.

"I'm sorry I got upset earlier," she said, almost mute. "It was a fight or flight response, and I was ready to do both."

"That's okay," I said, leaning down and planting a kiss on her lips. We hung together there momentarily, tenderly kissing, our hands exploring each other's flesh as we ardently made out.

"Mmm," sighed Henry, her hands slithering up my sides until they reached my breasts, lovingly fondling, caressing, her lower half grinding upwards against me. I could tell she was feeling good, primed for sex, blithely succumbing to passion.

"How about I lick you now?" I said softly against Henry's lips before giving her one more short, sweet kiss.

"Yep!" said Henry eagerly, nodding her head enthusiastically.

I slipped down the length of Henry's delicate body, kissing her navel, lowering, then kissing her hairless mound. While she had shaved herself clean, the tiniest amount of hair had grown back and gave my lips a bit of a prickle. I kissed around her mound for a moment, moving to her thigh, to her hip, and back again. I left subtly moist little marks with each puckered kiss.

"I'm so ready," cooed Henry, widening her legs, sighing happily. "I thought about you while I masturbated a couple times this week. Now I want the real thing."

"Oh yeah?" I said, my lips vibrating against her. I brought a hand up and began to gently massage her pussy, my fingers coursing over her, tracing some glistening wetness overtop of her beautiful, thin, buoyant slit.

"How does my pussy look without any hair?" Henry asked self-consciously, her eyes closed, her head falling to one side on the pillows.

"Beautiful," I said, giving her clit a slow, wet kiss, punctuating it with a smacking kissy sound.

"How do I taste?" she whispered.

Releasing my tongue, I ran it upwards over her pussy slit in a deliberate movement, collecting her creamy anointment on the tip of my tongue, tasting it further in my mouth, and once arriving at her clit with a slow slurp, I swallowed, tasting, smiling.

"Like gardenias," I said, moistly pressing my lips to her clit once again causing Henry to shiver.

"Mmm," she moaned contentedly, her legs coming up

off the bed slightly, knees in the air, spread for me. "Netty, will you do something for me?"

"Anything," I cooed, still kissing.

"Aw," she called, feeling my plump lips pressing into her little dewy nub. "Oh God," she said, trying to get her bearings, the pleasure she felt quite obviously going to her head. "When you're down there, will you... touch my... rear?"

"Like this?" I said, drawing my moistened finger down along her slit, running it over her taint, and finally landing on her tightly crinkled dot. I rubbed her rim in a slow circle, feeling the lightness of fine sporadic hairs between her cheeks. While she had shaved herself up front, her backside still had some thin fur, an adorable neglect that I found intensely arousing.

"Oh yes," she declared in an ardent whine. "Mmm, I love being touched there. It's so sensitive."

"You're so cute," I mused, rubbing my lips on her lips, the airy sweetness, the light stickiness of her pussy transferring between us. Licking my lips, I smiled, tasting again the floral sugar with just a hint of coppery bitterness. I absolutely loved the flavor of her sex. It was so intimate, so personal, so lush.

I buried my lips into her humid slit, kissing, licking, sucking, running my tongue up and down to eagerly taste her, then giving her the shivers and shakes by using my tongue to fondle her clit. While I attended to her milky flower with my mouth, her beautiful creaminess oozing out from inside and slowly running down, I used this moisture to rub her little rear knot in tender rings, joyously feeling all of the secret folds of tightly crimped flesh, breathing in the perfumed wafts from her underside, sensing my own heart quicken its pace along with Henry's judders and starts.

"Oh hell," Henry tweeted in a gentle tone, far away in a preoccupied dream, one hand resting on her breast, steadily moving up and down with her breath. My eyes aimed upward, I watched in awe as her little potbelly raised and lowered, my lips lovingly suckling on her clit. Henry was gone from this world, given in to the lustful excitation, her mind skipping stars while her body acceded to me. "Oh Netty," she moaned, short of air. "Oh my God."

With her labored and methodical breathing, I felt Henry's rear wrinkles part just slightly on each inhalation, my fingertip able to sense the very small opening of her backside fleck. I coordinated my finger with her breath and once I was sure of its timing, I eased my fingertip inside of her hole as it opened up for me. Once Henry felt this she bucked up off the bed, impossibly aroused, deep sounds emanating from her gaping mouth. I could feel her rim tighten around my finger, then loosen, and I very slowly, very carefully began to slide my finger back and forth while my lips kept focus on her sopping bloom.

"That's it," she advised in a rooted sigh. "Oh, that's so perfect." Her face looked desperately pleasured.

With another flick of my tongue against her clit, followed by a moist slurp, Henry started her convulsions. Her spread legs began to wriggle, one arm shot up and her hand gripped tightly to a pillow, while her other hand seized the sheets and held fast. Her midsection pumped up and down along with arduous grunting, and I could feel the rim of her ass clench against my inserted finger. Henry was coming and it spiced the aura around her pussy with a dendritic musk, causing me to go lightheaded with intoxicated passion. She was thrusting up off the bed, constricting my finger, exuding wetness, calling out my name. My heart was full, engorged, thumping with vigor inside of me. I was happy, so happy.

"Oh! I'm coming!" she moaned, trying to figure out what to do with her hands. She kept one hand amid the pillows and pushed the other one down onto my head, simultaneously bracing herself on me and lovingly petting me. With a smile on my face, I slowly removed my finger from her ass and pulled my face back from her pussy, intent to simply watch her writhe in orgasmic delight. I lifted my head and gazed up at her, meeting her eyes, and she gave me a loopy drunk smile as her hips fitfully thrust in irregular pushes. Placing a hand on her damp thigh, I tried to calm her with my smile, shushing her soundlessly with puckered lips. I was feeling stoned with love.

Once Henry's butt settled into the bed, her head rested back onto the pillows by her noodled neck, a sloppy grin across her lips, I slowly crawled up her body, sure to touch her along her midsection and sides as I moved. Reaching her face, I lowered myself down and placed a gentle, adoring kiss on her mouth, a kiss that she lazily returned. I heard her softly sigh and then slither a hand upward at me and under my arm, placing it cooly against my skin.

"Thank you," she cooed casually. I could only imagine

what was going on in her head, those little sparks of electricity, orgasmic aftershocks, one minute giving her clarity and the next minute making her lose track of time.

"You're welcome," I said, nuzzling my nose into hers, kissing her once again, easing my body down into hers to wrap her in a tender cuddle.

"I just wanna be in this bed with you forever," mused Henry, eagerly kissing me, letting her hands traverse my body. "Oh, thank you," she said again. The contentment was obvious on her face.

As we lay there together in post-coital bliss, I could think of nothing else but being with Henry, my adorable geek girl, unmoved by what anyone else thought. I had spent so much time seeking a relationship that wasn't right for me. I had become my own worst enemy. But once I was able to stop trying so hard and just let something like this happen, well, I was most certainly rewarded for my trust in the universe. With Henry and I snuggled together there in my bed, I felt a distinct change happening inside of me and I knew when I woke up the next day something would be different. I couldn't quite put my finger on it, just an intuition, just a vague notion that I had transformed in some way, like I'd been living in someone else's world for the longest time and I had finally been granted admittance to the world in which I belonged.

I closed my eyes. The smile wouldn't leave my face.

THE NEXT MORNING the two of us sat in my bed, a mug of steaming tea at the tables on either side. Henry was sitting upright, cross-legged, wearing only a little pair of green and grey striped panties that gave hint of her ass crack in the back, her small potbelly hanging over in the front just so. Her pierced breasts slightly hung down as she hunched over her laptop, fingers manipulating the keyboard and a wired mouse connected to the computer. She wore a headset over her ears, with a little microphone arm coming off of them, her glasses sliding down her nose as she stared into the laptop screen watching the colorful, cartoonish images move across the display.

I sat upright against the pillows, my Kindle in one hand and my cup of tea now in the other. I couldn't help but look over at her screen, watching her game as she played, interested by the focus with which she attended to it. I sipped from my tea as I watched.

"What are you doing now?" I asked, my eyes unmoving.

"I'm involved in a raid," she said. "It's a group of people, my guild, coming together for a joint mission."

"What's the mission?"

"We're fighting through this system of caves in a mountain, Killarney Keep, to get to the boss," she said, tapping away on her keyboard vigorously. My eyes broke from her screen for a moment to look at her chest, her beautiful breasts swaying slightly when her keyboard work became more heated, the little barbells at the nipples giving off the faintest of shine. I smiled happily to myself and returned my vision to her screen as she continued. "The boss is this giant ogre, just massive on screen. You'll see."

"It looks like your character is off to the side from the main fight, jumping around and such," I noticed, pointing at the laptop.

"I'm a 'Tree,'" she said, suddenly realizing that she was using some in-game slang. "Restoration Druid, I mean. I cast heal over time spells and keep an eye on my party over the course of the raid. Essentially, if other characters take damage I'm there to heal them."

"Oh, I get it," I said with a smile. "You do look like a tree. I wasn't sure what you were at first."

"Yeah," she mused. "Small laptop screen." Breaking her concentration she looked over to me and grinned, making a kissy face, before then returning to her task at hand.

"So you don't do the actual fighting?"

"Sometimes I 'Tank,'" she said. "Er, I go up front and fight a bit, but mostly take damage. Since I'm a skilled healer, it's no problem to take a bunch of damage and then heal myself."

"This all sounds pretty involved," I said.

"Nah," she said. "It's easy to get into."

Setting my Kindle and tea mug down onto my bedside table, I shimmied over closer to Henry, laying behind her against the pillows, but still propped up and able to see her screen. Absentmindedly I rubbed her lower back, sometimes letting a finger drop below into the gap between her underwear and rear.

"See," she said. "We're coming up to the boss."

"He is big," I marveled. "I mean, he takes up a huge amount of your screen."

"I know," she said. "It's much better to play on my large screen at home."

"So is this how you spend most of your Saturday mornings?" I asked.

"Yeah," said Henry, her typing becoming more intense, speedier, and her tree character bounced around the laptop display. "Really, a lot of my weekends are spent gaming. But maybe you can help change that," she said, looking to me, giving me a doe-eyed, affectionate face, and then quickly kissing me on the lips before returning to her screen.

"Maybe you could teach me," I said. "We could play together."

"Yeah?" she said excitedly, eyes popped open. "Oh wow, yeah, that could be a lot of fun."

"Sure," I said. "I could definitely use a bit of a diversion from work. It looks like there's a lot going on in the game, and I like thinking about a lot of stuff, multitasking, all that. I could get on board with gaming."

"That would be so hot," said Henry, eyes trained on her gameplay, her face twitching occasionally as something flashed on screen.

"Yes," I said. "But only if we break occasionally and have sex." I traced a single finger up her back causing her a tickle. Henry squirmed and laughed.

"Cut it out," she giggled. "I'm playing."

"You're so gorgeous," I mused, moving my hand up to her long brown hair, bunching it up, and pulling it back in a ponytail. Her neck was pale and slender, elegant, the perfect kind of neck to plant little kisses upon. She had little smatterings of light freckles on her white shoulders.

"Oh my God," said Henry, shifting a little bit in her cross-legged position. "It's like my brain is focused on the game but my body is getting excited for you. I'm getting, like, a little… wet… downstairs." I laughed happily at her.

"Well, maybe once you complete your mission," I said. "We can play a game of our own."

"I'd love that," she said. "You know what I love?" said Henry, turning toward me for a moment and ignoring her game. "I love when I get your juices all over my face and I can still smell your aroma, even after I've finished."

"Mmm," I contentedly intoned, rubbing her back. "I'm so happy about this… about us."

"Me too," said Henry. Quickly returning her eyes to the screen, she looked suddenly panicked as though she'd missed something in-game. "Oops!" We both laughed.

Just then I heard my phone vibrate against my bedside table. Sitting up and reaching to grab it, I looked down at the caller ID.

"Work," I said. "Blah."

"Screw 'em," said Henry.

"No, I should get this," I said, shifting out of the blanket and stepping out of bed. Wearing only a white tank and some thin pale blue short shorts, I stepped across the wood floor in my bare feet and made my way toward the bedroom door. "I'll take it in the hall," I said to Henry before walking out into the hall and pulling the door half-closed behind me.

After letting the phone buzz a few more times in my hand, hoping they'd just hang up, I sighed to myself and pressed the button to accept the call.

"This is Annette," I said into the phone with my business voice on.

"Netty, it's me," said Kate, her voice coming across as bitchy and hurried.

"Hey Kate," I said. "What's up?"

"Sorry to bother you so early on a Saturday," she said. "But we're hoping you could swing by the office this morning so we can get a leg up on this project."

"What?" I said. "This is pretty late notice."

"I know," said Kate. "It wasn't my idea, and honestly I'm a little too hungover to be productive," she admitted. "But Trevor received some corrected information about the new group's current funds and we need to change some of the language in our presentation."

"Kate," I said, shaking my head, entirely unenthused about the prospect of a hurried morning and weekend work. "You know I'm usually okay with Saturday work if something needs to be done, but I need some notice. I really can't come downtown this morning."

"Netty," she said, her voice becoming more serious and authoritative. "You can break whatever brunch plans you have. We need your input on this project. It's coming from higher up than me."

"I'm not even in Chicago," I lied, stepping up to my bedroom door and looking through the crack at Henry playing on her laptop. She was like an angel to me, sitting their half naked on my bed. "I'm out of town."

"You're with that geek girl, aren't you?" she accused. "You didn't even listen to what I told you."

"It's none of your business, Kate," I said. "It doesn't matter what I'm doing, I'm preoccupied and I can't get downtown."

"You probably drove up to a cabin in Wisconsin to build a fire and bump pussies," said Kate. "Or however that works." I couldn't help but laugh at her. "It's not funny, Netty," she said.

"Bump pussies?" I said. "C'mon Kate."

"You know what I mean," she said. "Trevor is not going to be happy about this."

"I'm just setting precedent," I said. "You can't call me on a Saturday morning and expect me to come in. I'm hours out of town."

"Just… fine," she said, fuming in a tantrum.

"Have a good morning, Kate," I said, unable to control my snark.

"Bye," she said, immediately hanging up.

I laughed to myself. I couldn't help it. Although I knew that this would get me into some trouble on Monday morning, I really didn't care to think that far into the future. I was content to live right now, to spend my time with Henry, who was so pure and so true. I wanted this to work out and I wasn't going to let my job get in the way of my love life anymore. So many relationships in my past had been ruined by my predisposition to do whatever my job said I needed to do. Work late, come in weekends, forsake living my life for the betterment of my work. There reaches a certain point in which money is no longer a tasty enough carrot to continue sacrificing yourself just to get more of it. I'm full of carrots, I've had my fill. I needed a greater meaning to my life, I needed to take care of my heart. Peering through the crack in my door, silently watching Henry, I felt almost dopey by my new pluckiness. This was a Netty I had known before and she was beginning to take back what was rightfully hers.

I was totally crazy for Henry, head over heels, and I knew this was something I wanted to last. No more fooling around. I knew I had done myself a disservice over the years by avoiding relationships with geekier girls, but there was no way I could get down on myself for it. Had I been a little more open minded in the past, I might not be here with Henry today. Things have a way of working themselves out and for that I am eternally grateful.

Looking up from her laptop and spotting my eyes through the door crack, Henry smiled at me and waved. She closed her laptop with one swift motion and removed her headset.

"Done!" she said. "Let's get intimate!" I watched as Henry threaded her fingers into the waist of her striped panties and slid them over her butt, pushing them down her legs until she reached her feet and removed them. Grinning at me, sitting there naked on my bed, she spun her underwear around on her finger until they suddenly launched off and flung to the floor. She laughed at herself.

My heart was full.

I stepped through the door and lowered my hands to the hem of my tank top, adroitly pulling it up my body and over my head, letting my breasts tumble out. Henry whistled at me and beckoned me with a single come-hither finger. Letting my tank drop from my hand, I slinked over toward the bed and crawled up onto it as Henry ruffled with excitement. She grinned widely as I leapt toward her, bounding on top of her, inspiring the two of us to roll around together on the bed, to laugh, to kiss, to love.

We all deserve to find happiness. And I was grateful to find mine in Henry.

Thank you for reading!

If you enjoyed this story,
please leave a review!

Reviews are *super* important!
Your review can help Nico
reach more readers!

Even if you're not the wordy type,
leaving a review saying
"I really enjoyed this book!"
is still incredibly helpful.

Pretty please?

If you want to be notified
of all new releases from Nico,
sign up for her mailing list today
and get a **FREE STORY**!

Point your web browser
to the following address
and sign up right now!

https://readni.co

Keep reading to see more books from
Nicolette Dane!

FIELD DAY

After getting into some trouble in the big city, Jane Cairns is sent to live with her aunt and uncle on the family farm. She's lost in life, worried, stranded, living in a state of arrested development as she ambles through her young adulthood. A normal twenty six year old woman should be able to flourish on her own, but Jane can't seem to make things work.

Farm life begins to show Jane a different side when she meets Sally Harris. Sally is a proud farm girl, in love with her country life, and happy to work at her family's cherry orchard. Things can be a bit stifling in the country, however, when it comes to love. And coming out from behind that barrier isn't something Sally knows how to do.

Each battling their own issues of identity and place, Jane and Sally struggle together to find out what it means to be free and happy. Will they be able to survive Jane's dirty past, secret love, family and friendship, and even death? Love is a tender and delicate thing, and it's something we all deserve. But the path to get there isn't always as straight as we might think.

TINY HOUSE BIG LOVE

After being laid off from her job at a law firm, Maxine Thune finds herself questioning her direction and looking for a change. She has lived out the typical life script. Max has the big house and the nice car, all the various trappings of material success, and she also has the debt to prove it. With this job loss, however, she's uncertain how she'll continue to afford it all.

But when Cadence Walsh comes into her life, the script is flipped for Max. Cady is a beautiful and free-spirited yoga teacher, she's a hippie, and she lives in a tiny house out in the woods. With no debts, few worries, and a more serene life, Cady reminds Max of her own bohemian past and she shows Max what their future could hold together.

Can Max ditch her life of over-consumption, learn to live small, and find tranquility in a tiny house? Will going tiny be the change Max needs to discover her authentic self? Just because a home is small, that doesn't mean the love within its walls can't be big. And sometimes removing what's unnecessary from our lives is the key to finding that which we truly need to grow.

FLOATS HER BOAT

After her mother's passing, Brooke Nilsson makes the trek up to her family's Minnesota vacation home to clean up the clutter and prepare the cabin for sale. Brooke never considered herself to be very outdoorsy, much preferring her big city life to lounging on the lake, and she's not looking forward to spending her summer in the middle of nowhere.

But when she meets her neighbor, famous singer Hailey Reed, Brooke's feelings begin to change about her old family getaway. Hailey, the beautiful and sultry redhead songbird, shows Brooke just how much fun lakeside living can be. And as the summer fun takes a romantic turn, Brooke can't help but question the way she's felt about the cabin for so long.

With a generous offer on the table, will Brooke be able to pull the trigger and sell her family's cabin? Or will her newfound love of the home, and her growing feelings for Hailey, prevent her from going through with the sale? Sometimes the stories we tell about ourselves are nothing more than stories, and our feelings about who we are can change when we least expect it.

GIVE ME SOME SUGAR

With the dream of owning her own bakery finally coming together, Angie West finds herself struggling with life as a business owner. She's overworked and underpaid, trying to figure out how she can take the bakery to the next level, balance all her money problems, and do so without sacrificing her mostly non-existent love life. Does an entrepreneur ever get a break?

Luckily, one of her customers is ready and eager to help. Ellen Liu runs her own business consultancy, the exact thing Angie and her bakery need. In addition to being bright, enthusiastic, and clever, Ellen is also a stunningly beautiful woman. And Angie, in a moment of weakness, finds herself kneading Ellen into a small fib to impress her biggest investor. Angie is totally smitten with her new partner, and it's coming out in the most half-baked way.

Can Angie get past her issues with family, money, and work, and allow love to prevail with Ellen? Will their relationship of convenience develop into much more than either woman thought possible? Or will this confection connection end up bittersweet? Angie's sure that Ellen's the one for her… now if only she can rise to the occasion.

GETTING DOWN TO BUSINESS

From the outside, Amy Barnes seems to have it all. She's a rising star at work, managing investor relations at a Chicago tech start up. She's well liked, she's funny, she's smart, she's pretty. But despite all this, for some unknown reason, she's had an absolutely awful love life. It couldn't possibly be self-sabotage, could it? It couldn't be Amy's fault, right? No way!

Enter Josephine Taft, rich and successful tech investor, swooping in to save Amy's company from financial ruin. In addition to being super wealthy and accomplished, Josephine is also a total fox. Will Amy be able to rein in her eccentricities to prove to Josephine that she's worth the investment? Or will navigating this conflict of interest prove to be too precarious for our quirky heroine?

As an often absurd Amy maneuvers through this stylized romantic comedy, always eager to get the girl, butting heads with a whimsical cast of characters, she just may discover that outward success isn't a good indicator of happiness inside. And sometimes, to prove our love, we've got to look within at our own inner truth. No sweat! *Right?*

RESTLESS ON A ROAD TRIP

Having just finalized the divorce from her husband, Dana Darling feels uncertain and lost in life. As a woman in her mid-30s, where does she go from here? How does she move on? Dana knows the divorce was the right thing to do and these feelings inside can no longer be ignored. She's certain real love is out there for her... but how can she find it?

When her good friend Maggie invites her on a road trip out west, Dana's eyes begin to open. Maggie is a firecracker, a sweet, pretty, and sensual woman who Dana has always admired. And while Maggie has always been open about her own love of women, Dana has never been able to come out to her friend and admit her true feelings. Dana is about to find out, however, that when you're on the open road with a fun and flirty woman like Maggie, things have a way of coming out like they never have before.

Will the freedom Dana feels on this road trip vacation allow her to finally open up and be free herself? Can this liberation from the responsibilities of life set Dana on the path she was meant to travel all along? Or will the coming out Dana has always deserved continue to be under construction? Some road blocks in life are difficult to navigate. But for Dana the call of the open road is too deafening to dismiss.

FULL BODIED IN THE VINEYARD

After yet another breakup and on the cusp of her 40th birthday, Shannon Laughlin is feeling lost. Life hasn't gone quite how she expected and she's ready for something new, a new outlook, a new adventure. A new love. One night, as she tries to figure out what's next, a chance post on social media by an old friend offers to give her that change she's been seeking.

That old friend is Alina. Alina is a seasonal worker at Wild Love Winery up on Leelanau Peninsula in Michigan's wine appellation. A free-spirited woman, Alina has orchestrated a life for herself that revolves around following her bliss. It's something Shan has always admired in her friend.

That, and Alina's undeniable sensuality. Shan can't help but remember the one night in college that the two women shared a bed. And the possibility Alina is offering is just too good to pass up.

Will Shan figure out how to get both her work life and her love life back on track as she stumbles into her 40s? Can the magic of Michigan's wine country and the surrounding beauty convince Shan that there's more to this world than she's been able to see? Or will this second chance at making it work with Alina prove to be out of her reach? Sometimes life is only just beginning at 40, as Shan is about to find out. And there's so much more of it to live.

AN EXCERPT: FIELD DAY

As soon as the bus pulled away, a cloud of dust in its wake, Jane reached into the back pocket of her shorts and pulled out a pack of cigarettes. She lit one up and inhaled, surmising the sprawling area in which she found herself. The bus station was at the corner where two big roads intersected. A gas station across the street. A bank to one side. It felt like the middle of nowhere to her. Jane exhaled.

Pushing a mess of blonde hair out of her eyes, Jane then adjusted her sunglasses and looked down to her duffel bag. It was army green, well-worn, and it had a couple of patches sewed on. She lightly kicked it and sighed.

"You really did it this time," Jane said.

Taking another long drag of her smoke, Jane caught the gaze of a man in his mid-thirties, about a decade older than her. He was checking her out as he walked quickly by. It was a hot late afternoon in the summertime and Jane wasn't wearing much in the way of clothing. The man was looking her up and down, though he didn't stop moving.

"You're drooling," Jane called after him. This brought a wry smile to the man's face.

"I'll use my tongue to lick it up," he said back at her, laughing now.

"Keep walking," she said. And he did.

Jane could feel the sweat lightly coating her forehead, beneath her chin, and under her arms. She wanted out of the heat. She wanted a shower. The air conditioner on the bus was broken, and she had been stewing in her own sweat for the entire trip from Chicago. The ride should have only been a few hours, but road construction in Indiana kept her in her seat for longer than she anticipated. Standing there at the station, Jane could feel a sense of unease. But she kept a cool look on her face.

After about ten minutes of waiting, and two cigarettes smoked, a late model pickup truck pulled into the station. Jane recognized this truck and she felt relieved. She lifted her duffel off the ground and watched the truck close in on her.

Inside the truck was a woman in her fifties, with kind eyes, her mousy hair back in a bun. She smiled as Jane stuck her head in through the passenger window.

"This ride go to the farm?" Jane asked coyly.

"Get in, missy," said the woman. "Toss your bag in the bed."

Jane smiled, and followed the order. Then she opened up the door and slid inside the truck.

"It's good to see you, Aunt Lori," said Jane, leaning over and wrapping an arm around the woman.

"It's good to see you, too," Lori said with a smile. "Now buckle up and let's get out of here."

Jane buckled her seatbelt like she was told and settled back into the cushion. Her aunt put the truck into gear, and then continued on, turning out onto the road and driving back in the direction from which she came.

"When was the last time you were out at the farm?" mused Lori, giving Jane a quick look before returning her eyes to the road.

"I don't know," said Jane, playing with her sunglasses. "I guess at least ten years or so."

"Probably longer than that," said Lori. "You got too cool to visit us."

"Not anymore, I guess," said Jane.

"Yeah, not anymore."

"Did Mom tell you everything?" Jane asked with caution.

"She did," said Lori curtly.

"She exaggerates," said Jane. "You know her."

"I know that my sister can exaggerate," said Lori. "But everything she told me definitely seems like stuff you'd do."

"Do you mind if I have a smoke?" said Jane, as though

AN EXCERPT: FIELD DAY

to change the subject. She was already reaching for her pack.

"Fine," said Lori.

Jane lit up yet another cigarette, taking a deep breath through the filter and exhaling out the open window.

"What are you…?" said Lori. "Twenty six?"

"That's right."

"Probably a little old to still be living at home," she said.

"I guess I'm not living at home anymore," said Jane.

"I guess not."

"Besides," Jane continued. "I was still taking classes."

"Sure," said Lori.

"I was," said Jane defensively. "I'm close to finishing my degree."

"Okay."

"How long till we get there?" said Jane, rolling her eyes behind her sunglasses, looking away from her aunt, and out at the passing trees.

"Just twenty minutes or so," said Lori.

"Is Uncle Bruce going to give me the treatment like you?" snipped Jane.

"I think your Uncle Bruce is just going to put you to work, dear," said Lori.

"What kind of work?"

"Collecting eggs," Lori said. "Feeding the horse. We've got a big lawn you could mow."

"I can do all that," said Jane. "Matthew's still kicking?"

"I don't know about *kicking*," said Lori. "But he's alive. We don't ride him anymore."

"I can feed Matthew," Jane mused. Pushing the cigarette to her lips, she took a long drag.

"Your Uncle will be glad to have your help," said Lori. "He's had a tough time recovering from his injury."

"I'll do what I can," said Jane.

"I know you will."

"Do you have a car I can drive?" asked Jane. "This truck, maybe?"

Lori laughed, and then stopped herself. She looked over at her niece and shook her head with a grin.

"You're something, Jane," she said. "We have a bike for you. That's it."

"A bike?" said Jane. "Okay, I guess that'll have to do."

"There's not many places you can go anyhow," said Lori.

"Town," countered Jane. "I could go to town."

"That's true," said Lori. "You can run errands."

"I'll do it," said Jane. "Will I get paid at all?"

"Get paid?" said Lori, laughing once again. "Lord, you're funny. Yes, you'll get paid something for your labor but don't count on making a mint."

"That's fine," said Jane. "As long as I can get a little something to walk around with."

"For smokes," said Lori, giving Jane a look.

"Maybe," said Jane.

Lori shook her head, her eyes remaining focused on the road ahead of her.

When they pulled up to the farm, memories flooded back to Jane. It had been years since she'd visited, but it was all so familiar to her. The house was white with black shutters, a huge antenna jutting up from behind it. There was a barn about fifty yards or so from the house, along with various other little out-buildings. And surrounding everything was a vast cornfield.

Jane thought she was in the middle of nowhere back at the bus station. But out here, she really *was* in the middle of nowhere.

When she was a girl, her family would come out to visit her aunt and uncle for long weekends. She remembered having fun running around the farm when she was young. She remembered a big forested area about a mile from the farmhouse, with a creek running through it. She remembered going into town and buying chewing gum from the hardware store.

But now Jane was an adult. She wanted to do adult things.

Once stepping out of the truck, Jane retrieved her duffel from the bed and hung it from her shoulder. She looked at the house and thought to herself that it wouldn't be so bad. It could be a lot worse. Her mom could have just kicked her out on the street, instead of sending Jane to the farm. This trip could actually be a vacation.

"Come with me," said Lori, motioning for Jane to follow her. "I'll show you to your room."

Jane followed Lori up a set of wooden stairs along the backside of the house, leading to a door. Lori opened the door and stepped inside. Jane went in with her.

The room was humid and stuffy, though it looked as

though it had been recently cleaned. There was an unmade twin-sized mattress on a wire frame, with a small wooden bedside table next to it. A dresser was pushed up against the wall to one side, a tall lamp adjacently positioned.

"Let's open a window," said Lori, walking across the room to one of the windows and opening it wide. "The screen will keep the bugs out."

"Thanks," said Jane, dropping her duffel to the floor and continuing to look around her new home.

"Don't smoke in here, okay?" asked Lori. "I know I can't do much to stop you from smoking, but just don't do it inside my house. We don't want any fires."

"Okay," said Jane. "I won't smoke in here."

"There are some sheets and such in the dresser," Lori continued on. "I just washed it all. You can make your bed and put your clothes away. I should go get supper moving along. We'll eat in about an hour, all right?"

"Sure," said Jane.

"Welcome to the farm," said Lori with a smile. Jane smiled back at her. Lori then walked toward the door, stepping back outside, and shut the door behind her.

Jane once again looked around the room. It was so quiet. Everything was so still. She wasn't in Chicago anymore.

"Hold the can," said Bruce, handing the empty coffee can back to Jane as he pulled open the screen door to the

AN EXCERPT: FIELD DAY

chicken coop. Limping inside, he held the door open for Jane and she followed behind him.

It smelled in the coop, and there were a couple dozen chickens inside the long room. Some of them sat on straw nests, some of them pecked around the floor. Jane looked around, wide-eyed, wondering if the chickens weren't about to team up on her and take out an eye.

"Each hen should lay an egg a day," said Bruce. "You come in here every morning and collect them in that can." He pointed to the can in Jane's hands.

"Okay," said Jane. "Then what?"

"Take them into the barn," he said. "We've got a bench over to the left when you walk in where you can put them. Every couple of days we have some people stop by to pick them up. It's $3 a dozen. We've got cartons in the barn, too."

"Wait," said Jane, lifting an eyebrow. "Don't they need to be refrigerated?"

"No," said Bruce. "Look here." Stepping forward, Bruce snatched an egg from one of the nests and held it up for Jane to see. "There's this protective coating over the egg that preserves it. If you wash the egg, it'll wash that coating away and then you have to stick it in the fridge. With the coating, it's fine sitting out."

"Wow, all right," said Jane. "So I just walk through and take the eggs?"

"That's right."

"The chickens aren't going to attack me, are they?" asked Jane.

"They might," said Bruce. "But you're bigger than them."

"Okay," said Jane. She took a deep breath and looked around the coop. It was pretty filthy, and very busy with the hens clucking around. But she steadied her nerves and started collecting the eggs with as much confidence as she could muster.

"See," said Bruce. "Nothing to it."

"What's my cut of that $3?" said Jane, grinning over at her uncle.

"Zero," said Bruce. "But I've got about a dozen other chores for you to do around here, as well. And I'll give you $50 a week for spending money."

"Okay," said Jane. "I can work with that."

Just then, a horn sounded off out in the driveway. Bruce perked up, and then shuffled past Jane and walked out of the coop. Jane picked up a few more eggs and put them in her can, but then her curiosity got the better of her. She followed her uncle outside.

In the driveway there was a pickup truck that looked like it had been ridden pretty hard over the years. As Jane stepped out into the light of the day, she saw a man get out of the passenger side of the truck. Bruce obviously recognized him, and the two men shook hands and began talking. Then, Bruce waved for the man to follow him and the two of them made off for the barn.

Inside the truck, sitting in the driver's seat, Jane saw a young woman. She couldn't quite get sight of the woman, but her interest was piqued. With the coffee can still in her hand, Jane walked across the gravel driveway and toward the pickup.

The passenger side window was rolled down and Jane stuck her head inside, resting the can of eggs on the window slot.

"Can I interest you in some eggs?" asked Jane. "Freshly stolen from the hens that laid them."

The young woman looked to Jane and smirked. She was pretty, tan, a brunette with her hair tied back in a loose ponytail. She had some freckles across the bridge of her nose and under her eyes. Sitting there in very short cutoff jean shorts and a tank top, the woman drummed on the base of the steering wheel with her fingers for a moment as she considered Jane's question.

"I can just get eggs from my own hens," said the woman. "Thanks, though."

"What's your name?" said Jane.

"Sally Harris," she said.

Jane thought for a moment, really focusing on the woman. It had been a long time, but Sally was familiar to her. She just couldn't place it.

"You're from around here?" said Jane.

"All my life," said Sally.

"I... recognize you," said Jane, narrowing her eyes. "Did we used to hang out?"

"Did we used to hang out?" Sally repeated. "I'm sorry, but I don't know if I've ever seen you before in my life."

"I'm Jane Cairns," said Jane. "Lori and Bruce are my

aunt and uncle. I used to come out here when I was a lot younger."

"Huh," said Sally, studying Jane's face and then looking her up and down. "That's familiar," she went on. "Jane."

"I just got here," said Jane. "From Chicago. I'm staying here for a little while."

"Get into some trouble?"

"You might say that," said Jane.

"What did you do?" asked Sally.

"It doesn't matter," said Jane. "But look, I'm worried I'm going to pull my hair out if I don't have some fun. Do you like to screw around and have a good time?"

"I might," said Sally, looking away and making a face like she was weighing her options.

"Maybe you could show me around town," said Jane. "Is this your truck?"

"It is," said Sally.

"Perfect," said Jane.

"Hold on," said Sally. "You think I'm just going to chauffeur you around town or something?"

"We'll hang," said Jane. "You drive us around..." she said, and then hoisted up the can of eggs. "And I'll make sure you get all the eggs you can eat."

Sally let out a short laugh.

"City girl," mused Sally. "You think you can hang out here? You know we party pretty hard in the country." Jane really couldn't tell if Sally was being serious or teasing her.

"I can hang," Jane assured her. "I can party."

"Okay," said Sally with a nod and a growing smile.

"How about I stop by here tonight around eight to pick you up?"

"Yeah?" said Jane. "That would be awesome. What are we doing?"

"If you can *hang*," teased Sally. "You can wait to find out."

"Fine," said Jane. "Whatever. I'm in. Let's do it."

"Eight o'clock," Sally repeated. "Don't dress fancy or anything. We're not going to some city club or something."

"I got it," intoned Jane, rolling her eyes. "I'll wear my daisy dukes and a plaid shirt, and I'll stick a corncob in my hair."

"I'll tell you where you can stick that corncob," snipped Sally with enthusiasm in her expression, her eyes darting to Jane's and locking on.

"I'm down with that, too," quipped Jane.

Sally grinned and nodded slowly. Jane grinned back.

"I only said the club thing because you look like one of those high maintenance pretty chicks," said Sally. "I hope you don't take offense to that."

"No," said Jane with a smirk. "I own it."

"Good," said Sally. "Looks like they're coming back." She nodded out towards the barn and Jane turned her head to look. Sure enough, the two men were making their way back toward the truck.

"Is that your dad?" asked Jane.

"Yep."

"All right," Jane continued. "You'll pick me up tonight at eight?"

"I will," said Sally.

"Cool," said Jane. "I appreciate it. I only just got here and everything feels like it's moving in slow motion."

"I get it," said Sally with a smile.

"Making friends?" asked Bruce as he and Sally's dad approached Jane.

"Yeah," said Jane. "Sally and I are gonna hang out tonight."

"Hmm," said Bruce, furrowing his brow.

"This your niece?" said Sally's dad with a grin.

"Yep," said Bruce. "Jane, this is Clyde."

"Nice to meet you," said Jane, shaking Clyde's hand.

"My girl can be a bit of a troublemaker," said Clyde, thumbing toward Sally inside the truck. Sally stuck her tongue out at him. "But she works hard."

"So's Jane," said Bruce. "But she's here to stay out of trouble."

"Yeah, but that's *city* trouble," said Clyde. "What harm can these girls do out here?"

Clyde's words circled around Jane's head. She could think of a lot of harm she could do. In the city, there seemed to be more accountability. Out here in the sticks, who would find out if she caused any trouble? Looking over to Sally, Jane tried to imagine her as a partner in crime. Maybe Sally was the type of girl who could be her new best friend. Sally had a knowing grin on her face, almost as though she could read Jane's thoughts. She delicately pushed a tendril of wispy dark hair out of her eyes, and then she broke from Jane's gaze.

"You keep an eye on this one," said Bruce into the truck at Sally. "I promised her parents I'd set her straight."

"Yes sir," said Sally with an impish grin. "You know me."

"I'll get that rototiller running and drop it by your place in the next few days, Clyde," said Bruce. He reached out, and the two men shook hands.

"I appreciate it," said Clyde. "You all take it easy."

"Will do," said Bruce.

Clyde climbed up into the truck and slammed the door behind him. With Sally at the wheel, they began backing out of the driveway, and then they were off. Jane and Bruce waved at them as they went.

"C'mon," said Bruce. "I've got this fence I want you to paint."

"Sure, Uncle Bruce."

AN EXCERPT: TINY HOUSE BIG LOVE

"Have a seat, Max," said Rich, my immediate supervisor at the firm. Along with him was Carrie, one of the partners, and Tina, an older woman who was the head of HR. I took a deep breath, pulled out the large leather conference room chair, and took a seat at the mahogany table.

"I can see where this is headed," I said, looking to each of them. I felt like I was going to be sick, but I knew I had to hear them out and go through the motions. These type of meetings had become frequent lately at our law firm. And they always ended with one of my long-time coworkers packing their things, walking out the door, never to be heard from again.

"As you know," continued Rich. "The firm has been struggling lately in this economy and we've been forced to do some downsizing."

"Right," I said.

While what Rich said was partially true, I also knew that the firm had been laying off senior employees, people like me who'd been with the firm for a while, and hiring recent graduates who they could pay peanuts. The firm *was* struggling, but there was still work to be done. The glut of recent law school graduates meant that a firm like ours could hire qualified people for very little money.

"These decisions haven't been made lightly," said Rich. "Management and the partners have really struggled with this, but we have to do what we have to do to keep the firm alive."

Yeah, I'm sure management and the partners have themselves made cutbacks and personal sacrifices to keep the firm alive. I didn't say that, but I wanted to.

"Unfortunately, Maxine," said Carrie stolidly. "We can no longer keep you on here at Harris, Stein, and Schusterman. We've certainly appreciated your service over the years, but we now have to part ways."

"We do have a generous severance package for you to sign," said Rich. He looked over to Tina, who shuffled through some paperwork and then handed him a contract. Taking it from her, he quickly looked it over, and then pushed it across the table to me.

I opened my mouth to protest, but then I thought better of it. I knew there was nothing I could say to make them change their minds. Lawyers had been getting laid off left and right, better lawyers than me, and none of them could save their ass with a few words at the conference room table. These decisions had probably been made weeks in advance. A lot of planning went into laying someone like me off. I'm sure my computer was being locked down by IT at that very moment. I was glad I had nothing personal on it. Never do anything personal on your work computer.

Looking over the severance package in the contract before me, my eyes started to glaze over. It was a boilerplate contract, very standard for the industry, something I'd read before as I'd worked on one similar for a client. It was generous, like Rich had said, but it also made me feel miserable. I had worked so hard at the firm, given them so much of myself, and now it was coming to a sudden end and I couldn't do a thing about it.

I nodded slowly and then I scrawled my name onto the contract. It was a sad moment for me, but I accepted it. There wasn't much else I could do.

With a security guard a few steps behind me, I exited the building holding a box in my hands. The summer sunlight hit my eyes and I squinted slightly. My bag threatened to slide down my shoulder and I scrunched up to keep it in place.

"Thanks Tim," I said to the guard. He nodded solemnly and then turned from me, making his way back into the building.

None of it seemed real. It felt like I was in a movie or something. Or a dream. Like it would all end at any moment. I'd wake up to the sound of my alarm, and then I'd jump in the shower, get dressed, eat breakfast, and head off to work. But it was none of that. This was my reality. I had been laid off from my job at the firm. I was only a lawyer now in credentials. I had no place to practice.

As I walked up to my luxury sedan, a glistening gray European automobile, I felt absolutely silly. How did I get here? Wearing a thousand dollar pantsuit, driving a fancy car, and now holding a box containing all my personal items from my office, leaving the firm for the very last time. I was closing in on my forties, and it felt like the past decade had been an absolute blur. Who the hell *was* I?

I opened the backseat of my car and shoved the box inside, then throwing my bag on top of it. Next I removed my blazer, folded it, and tossed it in the backseat as well. I slammed the door shut, I turned, and I leaned against the car, lost in thought. I crossed my arms over my white blouse, I pumped one of my heels up and down, and I felt like a fool. Nothing I had ever done seemed to matter at all.

Just then, from the front door of the building, I saw a woman exiting and breaking into as much of a run as she could in heels. She was in a light pink button down blouse and a grey skirt, her dark hair flapping in the wind, big black plastic glasses on her face. It was Ally, a young paralegal who often assisted me in my work. She made her way toward me, waving a hand in the air to try to get my attention.

"Max!" I heard her call out. I gave her a gentle smile and waved back at her, assuring her that I'd wait. Her run slowed to a quick amble, and it wasn't long before Ally approached me.

"Hi Ally," I said once she neared. She bent over for a moment to catch her breath. Ally was a cute girl, bright and driven. I'd always enjoyed working with her.

"Max," she said. "I just heard."

"Don't worry about me," I said. "Honestly, I was actually expecting something like this. There have just been too many layoffs lately and I was surprised I lasted so long."

"It's messed up!" said Ally. "You've really been an inspiration to me. You're one of the reasons I've decided to apply to law school."

"Really?" I said. "Wow. Thank you, Ally. That's sweet of you to say."

"I was wondering if you'd write me a letter of recommendation?" she asked cautiously. "I know it's probably weird timing, and I'm sorry for that."

"I'm honored," I said. "But it would probably look better if you had one of the partners do it."

"Yeah?"

"I'm just some unemployed lawyer now," I said. "I wouldn't have as much weight as some of the others."

"Oh," said Ally, suddenly looking as though I was really letting her down.

"I'll do it, though," I said. "If you want. But get a few others, too. And, you know, this is going to sound a little bitchy and out of place…"

"It's okay," said Ally. "I know how you can be." This candid honesty gave me a chuckle.

"Right," I said. "Well, I'd think really hard about law school. I'm sure you have already, but look at me now. I'm an accomplished attorney who did everything right and now... now I'll be replaced by someone at a third of my salary."

"Oh," she said, furrowing her brow.

"There are a *lot* of law school grads right now," I said. "Just be careful, Ally. All right?"

"All right," she said. "Thanks, Max."

"If you do want that letter," I said. "Give me a call. You have my number, right?"

"I do."

"Think about it a little longer," I said. "And then give me a call."

I smiled at Ally and placed my hand on her shoulder. She eased up a bit from my touch.

"Good luck," she said finally. "I know you'll be okay."

"Thanks, Ally," I said. "Get back to work, okay?"

"Okay, Max."

Ally gave me one more shy smile, then she turned on her heel and began walking back toward the office building. I watched her for a moment with a smile on my face, and sadness in my heart. I was honored that she had asked me to write her letter of recommendation, but I didn't want to see someone as smart and kind as her go down the same path I had traveled. Standing there next to my car in the parking lot, feeling more alone than I'd ever felt before, I could feel that my path hadn't lead me where I originally thought that it would.

I was a wanderer once again.

"A little more?" asked my older brother George, sitting across the dining room table from me with a bottle of wine in his hands. Next to him was his wife Lucy, a very pretty and affable woman with defined smile lines in the crooks of her eyes. At their behest, I'd come over for dinner and now we were relaxing at the table with some after-dinner drinks.

"Sure," I said, giving George a wave of my hand. He smiled and refilled my glass with Beaujolais.

"What do you think you'll do now?" Lucy asked, taking a drink from her own glass but keeping her eyes on me.

"God, I really don't know," I said. "The first thing that hit me when I walked in the front door this afternoon was the thought... how am I going to *pay* for all of this?"

"Your house?" asked George.

"My house," I said. "My car, my *bills*. I did a rough calculation of what my life costs every month, and now that I don't have my job... that number is *frightening*."

"You're not going to be kicked out of your house, are you?" Lucy said carefully.

"No," I said. "No, I mean, I'm *fine* right now. I am. I've got savings, I've got this severance. But the bills never end, even if the job does. Now I've got to figure out what I can do to stop the bleeding."

"I'm sure you can find another law job," said George,

AN EXCERPT: TINY HOUSE BIG LOVE

refilling his wine glass now. "There have got to be a lot of jobs in Grand Rapids."

"I don't know," I said. "I don't know if I even want to look for another law job."

"Wait," he said. "Are you saying you don't want to be a lawyer anymore?"

"I don't know," I repeated. "Ever since I got fired, a lot of crazy stuff has been flashing before my eyes. I'm questioning a lot of my life right now."

"I think that's to be expected," said Lucy. "Losing your job is traumatic."

"I got this strange feeling as I walked out of the office for the final time," I said. "That feeling was… freedom. All of the work stresses that I was constantly holding on to, they just immediately vacated my body. In fact, I couldn't remember the last time I'd felt so unencumbered."

"I get that," said George. "But that's a temporary thing. Like you say, you've got bills to pay. You've got responsibilities."

"It felt weird," I went on. "Like nothing mattered. Like nothing I had done in the past really made any difference. And while that might be depressing to some, it made me feel like… like I wasn't trapped. The world was opening up for me."

"Max," said George, shaking his head. "I remember this kind of talk."

"What's that supposed to mean?" I asked, lifting an eyebrow. Lucy looked at George as well with confusion on her face.

"Remember when you were younger?" he said. "You were a total hippie. You talked a *lot* about wanting to be 'free' of whatever it was holding you down that week."

"Oh, *c'mon*," I said with a short laugh, waving him off.

"You c'mon," said George. "Be careful with this line of thought, sis. You were kind of a lost soul before Dad pushed you toward law school."

"Law school worked for him," I said. "And he thought it would work for me."

"It did work for you," said George. "You've just hit a speed bump in your career. You're going to be fine. Don't think of this in terms of 'freedom' from whatever. No one's holding you down."

"No," interjected Lucy, giving George a skeptical look. "You're not giving Max the benefit of the doubt here. She just spent a decade working for a company that tossed her aside. She's allowed to have these feelings."

"She is," said George. "But I just want her to be realistic. Because I love you," he said to me in earnest.

"So what if I was a hippie," I said with a shrug. "And there's nothing wrong with questioning things around you, or questioning where you're at in life."

"No, there's not," agreed George.

"I'm only saying that I'm of two minds right now," I said. "On one side, I feel scared because of all these financial liabilities I have. And on the other… I'm feeling very free, very open."

"You know, something just popped into my mind," said

Lucy, raising a single finger up and looking to George. "I want to introduce Max to this woman I know. Her name is Cadence. Cadence Walsh."

"Really?" said George skeptically. "Cadence? You think she would be a positive influence on Max?"

"Cadence is a really free-spirited woman," Lucy said to me, ignoring George's protest. "I met her a while back at a yoga retreat. She's a total sweetheart, but she kind of lives outside the box. You know what I mean?"

"I'm not sure," I said. "What do you mean?"

"She's a hippie," Lucy admitted with a smirk. "But she's made it work. She seems really happy, healthy, just a good person all around. Maybe someone like her could help give you some direction."

"Is Cadence her real name?" I said. "That definitely sounds like a hippie name."

"I don't know," said Lucy. "All I know is that she's a really great woman and she seems to have life pretty well figured out. If you're feeling lost, it couldn't hurt to talk to her."

"Okay," I said. "Yeah, I'm game for anything."

"Oh boy," hummed George as Lucy and I continued on. I could tell he didn't think it was a good idea that Lucy connect me with her friend, but by that point there was nothing he could do to stop us.

"She lives out in Fennville," Lucy continued. "On a whole bunch of acres. Somewhere out in the woods."

"That's south of Saugatuck, right?" I said.

"Right," she replied. "I think she does some arts and

crafts stuff and sells it to the tourists during the summer, and that's enough to sustain her for the rest of the year. Plus she teaches yoga. I don't know how she does it, to be honest, but this woman doesn't seem to have a care in the world."

"Maybe she inherited a bunch of money," George broke in.

"I don't think so," said Lucy. "She definitely doesn't live lavishly."

"I'm on board," I said. "I think it would be interesting to talk to this woman and see what her story is. Maybe it'll give me a little insight into what I should do next."

"I'll dig up her phone number before you leave tonight," said Lucy.

"She has a phone?" asked George jokingly. Lucy laughed and smacked him on the shoulder.

"She has a phone," she confirmed. "Don't listen to your brother, Max. He's so pragmatic. I get exactly what you're feeling right now, and I think this is a great opportunity to explore yourself. Take some time and figure it out. You're not going to starve. You might as well have a little vacation from your problems."

"Yeah," I agreed. "This is an opportunity. It could be a new beginning for me."

"Take your time to figure things out," said George. "But don't give up on law. You've built a really good life for yourself."

"Yeah, for *myself*," I said. "It's just me. I've got this big house, all this stuff inside of it, and nobody ever sees it. I mean, what's the point of it all?"

"I don't know," said George. "But don't give up everything you've built. Talk to this hippie lady, see what the other side of the coin is like, but realize that you've got it pretty damn good, despite your current predicament."

"I'll take that all into consideration, bro," I said, giving George a wry smile.

"I think Cadence will give you some real insight," said Lucy. "She's such a positive woman, very giving and open. Maybe she'll remind you of what life was like when you were younger."

"Maybe," I said, still smiling now. I had no idea what this woman Cadence would be like, but the idea of her gave me a little bit of hope. Somehow I had found myself far down the expected life path, and it didn't feel like it was working for me any longer. Talking to someone who'd gone a different route, I think that could give me some perspective on where I'd been and where I was going. And if she turned out to be just some hippie burnout without any real insight, that wouldn't be so bad. Maybe she'd be pretty, too.

It had been a while since I'd been introduced to a woman. And although I didn't know what Lucy's full intentions were in connecting me with her friend, I sensed something in the way she spoke, and in the excited glimmer in her eye, that this introduction could be something a little more than just a friendly meeting between two people. Maybe it was wishful thinking, but I was feeling open to whatever the world wanted to give me at that moment. I had to be.

Made in the USA
Middletown, DE
16 October 2017